The Number of Missing

The Number of Missing

ADAM BERLIN

SPUYTEN DUYVIL

New York City

ISBN 978-0-923389-50-5

Library of Congress Cataloging-in-Publication Data

Berlin, Adam, 1966-
  The number of missing / Adam Berlin.
     pages cm
  ISBN 978-0-923389-50-5
  1. September 11 Terrorist Attacks, 2001--Fiction.
  2. Missing persons--Fiction. I. Title.
  PS3552.E724837N86 2013
  813'.54--dc23
                              2013005704

for John William Perry

Have you come here for forgiveness?
Have you come to raise the dead?
Have you come here to play Jesus
to the lepers in your head?

From *One*, U2

After dinner I take her to Angel's Share, a piece of Manhattan heaven two stories above street level where people say all kinds of things they'll forget. She's at the bar. I'm in the bathroom.

I've had a few drinks. Not enough though. Not enough because I'm with her and not alone. Not enough to smash my fists into something, hard, harder, the sad turning to anger, needing to get out the anger the way I can't get out the sad, needing to smash my fists hard and harder until something falls. That's one kind of falling. There are other fallings, hundred-story fallings, final fallings. And there's the fall you hope to get up from, the hope so great you actually hope you can fall all the way. But I can't fall all the way. She needs to fall first. It's the only good thing I do these days. I wait for Mel to fall.

So I don't make my hands into fists. I don't hit whatever's in front of me. I put water on my hands, cold water, and wash my face, press the cold into my eyes. I open them. Blink. Blink again. In the mirror I don't look grief-stricken. Things never change that much. And this city is big enough to hold grief. The hole downtown is still fresh, but the rest of the skyline looks the same and here in Angel's Share with its low lights and slow-rhythmed music even love seems possible.

I walk back to the bar. The bar itself is sleek and polished and long enough to support the arms of many strangers. The bottles of alcohol, doubled by the mirror behind them, have been wiped clean and carefully arranged. I sit down next to Mel. She smiles at me like she's seeing me for the first time tonight.

"So how did you find this place?" Mel says.

"A woman took me here."

"She must have liked you. This isn't the kind of place you take just anybody."

Mel looks around.

"Angel's Share," she says. "What a name. It's the kind of place you keep secret for as long as you can."

Mel orders an Old Fashioned and the Asian bartender goes to work, his head bent, his mouth set, the movement of his hands strong and crisp as if he's working with solids instead of eighty-proof liquids. When he's done he places the drink in front of Mel and nods his head once, formally, for her, for himself, for the drink. The final product is more potion than cocktail.

I order straight bourbon. It requires a simple pour into a simple glass without any distractions. I count the alcohol going in.

Mel lifts her drink, sips. She puts the glass down and I watch her tongue take a final drop of whiskey off her top lip. She's not in a rush to do anything these days.

"Well," she says and the way she says it, so neutral coming out, doesn't mean she likes it or dislikes it.

"In a place like this the world almost seems far away," Mel says.

"I guess that's the point."

"I guess it is," she says.

Then a cell phone goes off and we're back in the world.

"No escape," she says.

A man farther down the bar, his beret cocked at an exaggerated angle, speaks too loudly, broadcasting for everyone the monumental dilemma about whether his friend should meet him here or if he should meet his friend there.

"Thanks for filling us in," I say, but the man doesn't hear me.

"Meet your friend there," I say, pretending to talk to him, but joking for Mel, trying to keep the world at least a little far away. "Since you're wearing a beret and since you're including us in your scintillating conversation, I'd like to cast my vote. Put me down for there. Let's make it official."

"It's official," Mel says.

The man closes his phone but stays seated at the bar. He sips from a colorful drink. He lights up a cigarette and keeps the cigarette between his middle and ring fingers and I wonder how long he practiced his practiced move in the mirror.

"I guess my vote doesn't count," I say.

"So what sorts of women do you usually bring here?" Mel says.

"Women who can keep a secret. I wouldn't want the

word getting out to the beret-wearing crowd."

Mel's mouth appears so relaxed she seems on the verge of smiling. It's an expression that reassures people who don't look closely, but her mouth is also mysterious, the width of her lips, the space in between a hint at something darker. I'd noticed her mouth the first time I met her. And I'd noticed her eyes, the lightest blue, and alive, moving here and there and then staring straight on. And now there's darkness under her eyes like she hasn't slept well for too many days, almost like someone punched her just hard enough to leave a little black, a quarter-moon smudge under each eye.

"The woman who brought me here the first time told me this was the kind of place you should bring someone special and since she was the one who brought me here, I figured she knew what she was talking about."

"Who was this woman?"

"Just a woman. She wasn't the kind of woman I would have brought here if I were following her advice. But I'm glad she brought me. It's a nice break from the usual places I hang out."

"It's not like you ordered anything different."

"No. But he poured a full three-count of bourbon so I can't complain."

"Well," she says.

"He was so happy he didn't have to make a specialty drink, he rewarded me for my easy order."

Mel almost smiles. Her eyes look past me, looking from one drinker to the next and then back to me, steady. When she focuses on a person, when she gives full attention, it is full, like there's no one else she'd rather talk to. She takes another sip of her Old Fashioned. Her fingers against the glass. Her wedding ring the color of whiskey.

"Did you stand today?" she says.

"I stood."

"Any good artists in the class?"

"I don't know. I try to think of other things when I'm standing there. It helps me hold the position and it makes the time go by."

"Maybe I should do what you do," Mel says.

She takes another sip of her drink. She looks around the bar. I look at the fine muscles in her neck, at the two points of her clavicle. Her grief has not so much changed her as stripped her down, stripped her body and her face. Maybe she should do what I do. She could stand next to me and the students could draw our lines. I order another bourbon, count the count.

Angel's Share starts to get crowded. All the barstools and tables are full and the people coming in stand behind the stools, waiting for someone to leave, holding their drinks close to their bodies so they can dash to the first vacant seat. Another bartender comes on, also Asian. He makes drinks just as meticulously. There isn't a tap anywhere near the place and if there were, I wonder what kind of production they'd make out of pouring a beer. Angel's Share. It really is a nice place to bring someone you care about. Sometimes it really does separate you from the world, which is what the alcohol is supposed to do on its own but doesn't always. And hidden behind a nondescript door, Angel's Share seems like a discovery. It's a break from the usual, but the usual isn't bad, no bar is bad after the fourth or fifth drink and the warmth takes over, makes you forget, makes everything seem possible, irresponsibly so.

We finish our drinks and leave Angel's Share, walk down the stairs, onto the street. Mel keeps her back to downtown. We walk up Third Avenue for a while. She has very good posture. Her stride is long and straight and she keeps her eyes straight ahead so when I talk to her I don't even bother turning my head.

"Do you have a busy day tomorrow?"

"Not too busy," she says.

My hands are fists. From the cold too, I guess.

"Things are slow everywhere," she says.

"They are."

"We may get a new client," she says. "A new cosmetics company that wants to launch a major campaign but doesn't have the money to launch a major campaign. The CEO is a kid really, but he's a real dreamer and always thinking big. What about you?"

"I'll take a run. I'll go to work. The usual."

"And then you'll go out."

"Maybe."

"But not to Angel's Share," she says.

We're at the subway stop, the green globe lit, the station open. It's our third time out and this is what we do. We go to a bar, we talk but mostly don't talk, and then I walk her right to the station but don't go down the stairs with her, as if that would mean too much. I can't get on the subway with her. I can't walk her home. I can't kiss her at the door, a real kiss. I can almost see Paul next to me, smiling. Not a jealous smile but a real smile. The smile he had for Mel. The smile he had for the city. We walked the streets so many late nights and he'd look up, always looking up, and I'd follow his eyes and look up at all the lit buildings, so light they made the stars disappear. His nights in New York never had a downtown hole. Mel stops, keeps her back to downtown.

"Thank you for the drink," she says.

I smile and she almost does, maybe.

"I didn't mean that," she says.

"So you don't want to thank me for the drink?"

"No. You know what I mean. It sounded so formal. *Thank you for the drink.*"

"That's okay," I say.

"Thank you," she says. "For taking me out. It's nice to have something to do after work. People call. My family calls and people at the office invite me out to dinner. But if I were with them, I'd have to work too hard. With you, I don't. Sometimes it's nice to just sit somewhere else for a while."

"Good."

"So thank you."

There's really nothing else to say. Good-byes, when you can say them, always seem like the time to say things, to sum things up, as if that were possible, put a nice cap on things.

Mel leans in and kisses my cheek and I kiss her cheek and her almost-smile goes away and her eyes look at me, like I'm the only one around but I'm not, and then she's walking down the stairs.

I walk downtown. It's a cold fall night. I lost my gloves last week on a drunken night out and haven't bought new ones. I called the bar where I'd been, I'd remembered that much, left a message for the lost-and-found person, but no one called back. I could have left the gloves somewhere else, there had been bars before and bars after, and I could have just dropped them on the street. Pieces of nights are blacked out these days, and the next day, sick in bed, the headache behind my eyes and my stomach craving meat to soak up the booze in my blood, I go over the skipped moments, trying to connect the dots, figuring out how I got from there to there to there. Like replaying a trip. It's the only escape I know. These nights I go out every night. These nights.

I see a bar, look through the window, go in.

I was sitting in Father Demo Square the morning of September 11th. I'd just finished my run, down to the World Trade Center and back. It was a beautiful morning, sunny and warm and one of those Manhattan mornings where the air is almost fresh and the light so perfect the city's lines are straight-edged, the kinds of lines architects must dream.

The pigeons were out in full force as they always were in Father Demo Square. These pigeons, like the people who hung out in the square for more than an hour at a time, were beaten up by the city, scrawny and scrappy, hungry enough to be bold, come right up on your lap if your lap held a pizza crust or the end of a sandwich. A homeless man sat sleeping two benches away, head fallen against chest, mouth open and relaxed, a line of dry spittle in his beard. The old Italian women sat on the benches closest to Our Lady of Pompeii, gesturing and shaking their heads too emphatically to be talking about the morning's mass. Traffic was already steady, going uptown. It wasn't quite rush hour. It was primary day and a man on the corner was handing out political pamphlets.

I heard it first. Planes flew over the city all the time, but they usually flew south to north, then circled around Manhattan's top tip in their final approaches to LaGuardia. I heard the jet engines, that mourning, moaning sound they make, yearning to speed over the landscape just a little longer, not come down. The noise became too loud. The pigeons lifted off and flew in one direction, then another. I looked up. I had never seen a plane that close to the ground. Never, unless I was actually at the airport. It looked like the plane was making its final approach, an American Airline landing on the Avenue of the Americas. As if Sixth Avenue were some mid-city runway. It didn't look right. It didn't look real. I stood, automatically, the back draft of something wrong lifting me off the bench and setting me down in the middle of the avenue to watch. And I watched. I watched the plane move low over the city, too low, and there were the two square spikes that held Manhattan down, that secured the lower half of the island, square and strong, so much a part of the skyline they were part of every person's memory who had ever flown over New York at normal altitudes.

It didn't make sense. A plane flying this low.

The jet engines moaned and then the moans blended into the sounds of the city, became part of the background noise, and the plane's background became the two towers and then the one tower. There comes a point when you can't get out of the way, when mathematical equations that calculate speed and distance make it physically impossible to escape, when the line is fixed, the course inevitable, and only the hand of God can snatch the moment, make it not happen. It couldn't be happening, but it was.

The plane went straight into the North Tower.

Fireball.

Smoke.

I was running downtown.

I tried to count, head straining forward, breath hard in my chest, running harder than I'd ever run, as if I were being chased, but really the terror was so great it was chasing me, in front of me but forcing me to run. I tried to count down the floors through the smoke, to see if he was in the middle of what had to be an inferno inside but from outside looked like a hole with some fire around it. The smoke was more spectacular, already arcing over Brooklyn, wide and gray and thick, a devil's rainbow. I was running and trying to count down the floors to Paul's office on the 103rd floor. I was close to the tower but not close enough, not close enough to help him if he could be helped. The cops were keeping people away and one cop grabbed me and told me not to be stupid, not to be a hero, to stand back and wait. The cop had kind eyes. And his eyes were scared. I stopped. He wasn't giving orders. He was talking to me. He was telling me to wait. I was telling him my friend was in the building. He was telling me to wait, that they would do what they could, that I couldn't do anything, that there were already hundreds of firefighters at the scene and he told me just to wait.

I waited. And waiting, I watched. I watched the fire coming out of the hole. I watched the smoke arcing over the river. And worse. I watched the bodies falling, far enough away where they had no personalities attached to them. Just bodies falling through the air.

The people moving past me were crying or numb-faced. Soot-stained. Pieces of burnt paper in their hair.

I turn the water all the way hot, turn my back to the water, and I take it. I close my eyes and I'm on the hundredth floor with the jet-fuel fire at my back and the drop below.

I take it and take it until I can't take it, until the heat takes over everything, and I jump, plummeting to the street.

I'm out of the shower.

I turn my back to the mirror and look at the too-red skin between my shoulder blades. The wind blows north and the smoke is here. Then the wind shifts and you can't smell a thing. Then the wind shifts again. Now you smell it, now you don't.

Garrett Shane went to my high school in Massachusetts, but I didn't know him there. He was two years older than me, two class corridors away, beige to green to blue. I only knew Garrett the way everyone in the school did. His older sister had left town, moved to Seattle and made it as the lead singer in a grunge band. Her face was all over TV and magazines. Garrett's face was never on TV, but when I saw him at an uptown bar I recognized his face. He came over to me, told me I looked familiar and I told him I knew him from high school. Garrett looks like his sister in his eyes and nose, but she's wiry-thin in her music videos while he's thick, years of good living stretching his waist. Garrett made a quick killing on a case his first year out of law school. Two dozen factory workers had suffered brain damage working with excessively toxic paint. One third of the settlement, the standard lawyer's cut, made Garrett rich.

Garrett's doorman knows me from many nights out.

He lets me walk right through, right across the lobby's polished stone tiles. Garrett lives on the twenty-first floor with a view of Central Park. A new skyscraper is going up and his piece of green and trees will soon disappear if the building continues, which it will, if people put their nightmares away to live on high floors, which they will, if life goes on, which life will. Garrett's door is open so I walk in.

He has a great apartment. Full living room. Separate bedroom with a king-sized bed he's slept alone in almost every night since he bought the place. His bathroom is more modern and comfortable than any place I've ever lived, with state-of-the–art fixtures, marble tiles and plush bathmats vacuumed by his twice-a-week cleaning woman. My apartment's floor slants at such a steep angle I practically need a pickaxe to walk its length, a few feet of square footage. My bathroom has broken tiles, bad grouting, a stained mirror, a rusted radiator that hardly works. My bed, bureau and table fill most of the space and my miniature closet is full even though I've pared my clothes down to a minimum. Officially, my apartment is called a Rooming House room like I'm just passing through, which is how I felt before I met Paul and, now that he's missing, I feel again.

Garrett is on the phone. He nods his head and points to the alcohol. I take a rocks glass and ice and pour myself a four-count of Maker's Mark, with long *ands* in between the numbers. Garrett's already working on a bottle of Belvedere vodka he keeps in his stainless-steel freezer. Garrett likes the best of things and his one big settlement allows him to buy the best. And Garrett is a generous man. I appreciate his generosity even if I've warned him to avoid being so generous with careless people.

The phone conversation is business, something about a last-minute deposition that hasn't been completed. On his flat-screen TV, the Yankees are running into the field to start a new inning. I change the channel to CNN. Terrorism is still the number one item. There's a long shot of Afghanistan's mountains and then a shot of people in a city market and then a shot of men training. Their faces are covered and they're holding guns and running in the sand. I lift my arm, point my index finger at the fuckers on screen, say *Bang*.

Garrett gets off the phone and we start drinking. He tells me about a woman he met and how they hit it off and how she invited him out to D.C. for a date and how he bought a plane ticket and booked a room at the Four Seasons and then, three hours before departure time, she called to tell him she'd gotten back together with her boyfriend.

"So how was D.C.?"

"Very funny," he says.

"You'll meet someone else. New York's full of someone elses."

"Three hours before departure time. What if I'd been on the damn plane?"

"Then you would have seen the view."

"I'm a good guy," Garrett says. "I'm a nice guy. I'm always polite and respectful. But three hours? I don't understand women. The new me is going to be a selfish bastard."

I finish my drink. It gets in my blood that fast.

"The new you?"

"That's right."

"Since September 11th?"

"All right. I know it's trivial. I know it's just a girl. I didn't even know her, but still."

"*I hate myself for it. Because I don't want the girl, and, still, I take it and—I love it.*"

"What's that?"

"Nothing. A line from a play."

Garrett pours himself a Belvedere.

"The new me," he says.

"How have you changed?"

"I've changed."

"Tell me."

"What do you want me to say?"

I look at Garrett to see how long it will take him to break eye contact. One and two and. He moves his eyes. He didn't know Paul the way I knew Paul. But everyone's back to life too fast.

"Fill me up," I say.

Garrett takes my glass.

"All right," he says. "All right. We're going out. We're hitting the town tonight and forgetting about everything."

"Bourbon."

"I'll never make another flight reservation to see anybody. I'm strictly local from now on."

"A little more."

"Strictly local."

He hands me the drink and I gulp it down and he pours me another.

I wait for time to start skipping. Skip me past sadness. Skip me past the recent past.

I drink down. He drinks down.

We leave Garrett's apartment. The doorman gives us a mock salute, wishing his troops well in the field of battle. It's a bullshit battle. It isn't about life and death. It's about forgetting life and death.

Time skips. A small skip. I'm out. With Garrett. With his wallet full of money. With my wallet as full as I allow myself to fill it. These careless nights out are expensive, but inevitably I'll end up drunk at some bank machine, calculating the number of drinks per twenty dollars, or when I'm really gone I'll hand the bartender my credit card and start a tab I'll regret when I'm sober. There's one good side to these late-night, recorded transactions. They help me fill in some blacked-out spots, and when I'm too beat-up to drink I replay them, a concentration game, drunken memories helping me forget the missing.

I point to the window of a crowded bar.

"Here."

We've been here before. It's standing room only, but there's enough room for two more bodies to squeeze in.

"I better get laid tonight," Garrett says.

I open the door.

We're in.

We're at the bar.

We're drinking.

Time skips.

I leave Garrett somewhere, some time, and I'm in the street. I'm seeing the explosion. I'm seeing the smoke. I'm Paul, looking out the window, fire at my back, steel cliff at my feet, wondering what to do, what to do, what to do. I don't know what to do.

Time skips.

Skips again.

And again.

A bar. I'm talking to a woman. She's writing her number on a napkin. I'm talking to another woman. I make a muscle for her, ask her to feel my arm. I'm laughing. I'm walking with a woman. Getting in and out of a cab. I'm in a woman's bed. Moving. Time skipping. A garbage truck stops, crushes, starts. I get out of bed. I get out. A subway ride. Me relying on the me that always gets me back.

My bed.

I wake. I'm thirsty.

I wake. I spit dry spit.

The phone rings. Sun's coming through the blinds. The machine picks up. It's Garrett, calling to make sure I've gotten home safely. I'm home, so I have. I pick up the phone and Garrett asks what I ended up doing so he can get his thrills vicariously.

"No luck?" I say.

"None. What about you? What sordid details do you

have for me?"

I tell him my night's story, put it together for him, dot by dot, fragment by fragment. I fill in the parts I don't remember with what must have happened.

"You looked pretty fucked up last night," he says.

"I know what I look like. I see what I look like in the mirror."

"That's great," Garrett says.

"I need these nights out."

"I know it's been hard for you."

Garrett can be kind and there's care in his voice, like he knows about hard things. Maybe it's because he never lived up to his sister's fame. He doesn't like to talk about her, but sometimes when he's drunk he lets it slip how his parents are more interested in her career than his, her life than his.

"Everyone needs these nights out," I say.

"Take it easy today," he says.

I don't say anything.

"You there?" Garrett says.

"I'm hungover. I'll talk to you later."

My head hurts.

My stomach's empty raw.

My heart's too fast.

The checklist of damage.

I stay in bed looking at the ceiling.

I'd like to run. Run and run and run. Paul wouldn't have run. But maybe I'm wrong. In a real war, no one knows how he'll react until it's happening. There's a war on, sort of, but unlike some Hollywood hero who defends his fellow men in trouble, saving everyone in the foxhole before he saves himself, I want to run alone. But I can't run alone. She's here. And he's here. He's almost that alive. The three of us in the mud.

I need a drink. I'm not a soldier. I could play a movie soldier, like the soldier in dreams. In the dream you survive. You always survive when you think about going to war, fighting, winning, returning the hero. If you don't survive, you can't tell the story. But in real wars, real attacks, bodies burn, bodies fall, bodies disappear.

There's still alcohol in my blood. I can almost pretend I'm back in time. Back in false dreams. Soldier. Running. Light. Carrying just enough to move quick and easy and alone, fast, fast, fast.

I stand.

They draw.

The trick is to think about something far away so your muscles don't cramp. Before it was my nights out with Paul. Where we went. What we did. Now it's after. I see him and it's hard to see him at the same time. When I try to focus on his face I can't see it. Only when I see the larger picture, as if I had to look from the side, *by indirections find directions out*, can I see him, all of him, eyes to nose to mouth to neck to body and then I don't look so closely at him but at the two of us together, living moments. The instructor tells me to change position. So I do. The new position highlights different muscles, creates different lines.

Sometimes when I step off the platform I see what they've drawn. It's my body in all of them. But not really. I have as many different bodies as there are artists in the room. In every class there's usually one with real talent and in those drawings my body is the most different. In those drawings it's my body, but the artist is in the lines that define my limbs. The lines become more important than my limbs. Me but not me.

I listen to the ringing, a sort of private siren turned all the way up in volume. By now everyone who used to call knows I don't answer my phone but listen first and not wanting to be on the receiving end of a harsh decision to not pick up, they don't call. Women I don't know call. I'm too quick to give out my number when I'm drinking. When they call, I press erase.

I listen to the last ring, listen to the machine kick in, hear her voice, pick up.

"I'm here."

"Still screening?"

"Busted."

"I'm just calling," Mel says.

"Good. Good. How are you?"

"I'm fine," she says and laughs.

"I'm a little drunk," she says.

"You never get a little drunk, do you?" she says.

"Are you at work?"

"I didn't go in today. I didn't feel like going in. I felt like taking a long walk. The air was so crisp it felt like sharp angles in my lungs. I walked all the way uptown, and then I took a subway back. Did you run today?"

"I ran."

"That's even harder."

"I don't know. I just force myself to run."

"Even when you're hungover?"

"I try."

"You're hungover a lot, aren't you?"

"*I am what I am*," I say, my voice, Popeye the Sailor Man's words, flex my arm for myself and imagine Popeye's obscenely pumped forearm, anchor tattoo, a proud member of the navy. Army. Navy. Airforce. Marines. The commercials have started, slick and romantic, all the uniforms crisp and too clean, the music so rousing it's like a movie, the beginning of a movie where everything seems possible, where you can feel the life you want to live before a bad line or an exaggerated gesture makes it false. I'd take the land. Popeye would take the sea. I can't think of anyone for the air. There wasn't anyone protecting the air when they turned our planes to missiles. I could hit something, but I don't know what.

"I'm not."

"You're not what?" I say.

"I'm not what I'm not," Mel says and then there's a beat of silence. "I'm just not."

"No one is."

"I'm a little drunk," she says. "I woke with a hangover, so I had a drink. You know the trick."

Hair of the dog, I want to say but don't. Her voice is not really her voice. It's a note higher, on whatever scale voices are. Her voice is usually low, lower in her throat. Paul loved her voice. He said she sounded like she smoked, but she didn't, and it wasn't an act. Paul had a good voice. And he could sing. When we drove across country together, windows down, radio loud, he'd sing along to the songs he liked. Mel sang too on the rare times the three of us drove together. It's not her voice now, singing or speaking.

"Do you ever start in the morning and then keep going?"

I want to say that I haven't been drinking, that I don't let myself drink so much since it happened, but she'd know it's a lie. She knows about time-skips. She was married to him and now he's not here. She needs drunk time-skips more than I do.

"You know how I drink," I say.

"How do you drink, David?"

My name in her mouth. It's not her voice, not the voice I know, but it's her mouth. I can see the space between her lips and the darkness behind.

"I drink at night," I say. "I binge drink."

"That sounds like fun."

"It's a lot of fun."

"Then why do you do it?"

"To have fun. To wake up with that fun feeling pounding in my head."

"Well," she says.

"Do you want to take another walk?" I say.

"I already took a walk."

"We could take a walk together."

"I already took a walk. It's better to take those sorts of walks alone. I just called to say hello. I just called, you know."

"Do you want to get something to eat?"

"No." She starts laughing.

"That was honest of me," she says.

"*In vino veritas.*"

"He used to say that all the time."

"I got it from him."

His lines are my lines are our lines we go that far back. That far back. Time is so fucked up back is forward and present is past and two towers disappeared, now you see them, now you don't. He's dead. She's drunk. It will be night soon. I'll be going out soon. Binge drink to sunrise.

"Hello?"

"I'm here," I say.

"Don't be angry at him. I'm angry at him sometimes, but when I catch myself I know how wrong that is."

If she could take a cross section of my balls she would

see the anger there, too much anger to dismiss, too much to drink away. The anger at him replaced by the anger at myself for not making things right before he was killed replaced by the anger of helplessness, unable to stop two planes from flying into two buildings. And the sadness. The sadness that takes over the anger like palm-paper covers fist-rock in a child's game.

"It's wrong," she says but not to me.

"You should eat something. That's another trick for you to keep those hangovers away."

"I'm not hungover now," Mel says.

"Are you going to work tomorrow?"

"I'll think about it," she says. "It's funny. You take the day off and do nothing and it goes by so quickly. It seems to take the whole day to buy some food, to cook a little, to do some small chores. I don't know where I find the time when I'm working. I don't know where anyone finds the time."

"Time doesn't work the same way these days."

"It's too fast and then it's too slow. It's too slow at night.'

"Call me when it gets too slow. Or too fast. You can call me whenever you want. You know that."

"Can you change the pace of time?"

"I can try."

"But you can't change time."

I don't say anything.

"He hated that you didn't speak to him for so long. He wanted you to know how he felt. What was so wrong with that?"

"Nothing was wrong."

"He wanted more for you," she says in her voice that's not her voice. I hear ice against glass and then a sip.

"He said you kept everything separate," she says. "What you did and what you wanted and how you acted with different people and even your drinking. He just wanted the lines to blur a little for you. Not the drinking. He didn't want you to drink so much. The other lines. He wanted all the separate things to be not so separate. He didn't think you were really living. He didn't think you were content about anything and he was worried about you."

"No more worries."

"It's not the way to live. It's living in pieces and not really living."

"He already told me that."

"That's why I said it. That's what he told me about you even before you fought. Don't worry. Paul kept you private in a good way. That's how I knew you were such close friends. The night he came home after you fought, he couldn't sleep. I asked what had happened and he shook his head. He could hardly talk. All he said was he had talked to you about you."

"My favorite subject."

"It wasn't your favorite subject that night."

"I didn't feel like listening about me."

"That's what close friends do. They talk and they listen. That's what they do."

"I didn't know the rules."

"There aren't any rules."

"Not these days."

"No," she says. "Not these days. But I'm talking about no rules in a good way. There aren't any rules with friends."

We had fought. I had run. He was killed. I hear ice against glass, then the sip.

"He wanted you to be a better you," she says.

"Remember that," she says.

"You remember that," I say.

"I do remember it. Every day."

"You want to hang up, don't you?" she says.

I'm pressing the phone hard against my ear. I catch myself and ease it away. I can hear her breathing.

"I'm here," I say.

"*In vino veritas*," she says and sips.

"He wasn't a saint," she says. "He wouldn't want us to romanticize him that way. But I was a better me after I met him. When I was with him, I was a better me."

I can hear Mel go away. I can see how she must look, her head down, her hair falling over her eyes, her eyes not all there she's so far away with Paul. He wanted me to be a better man. He wanted me to break the lines that separated my life. My ambition to be seen, to be a star, things I didn't really love. My relationships with women I didn't care about. My drinking those extra drinks after he stopped drinking for the night. Craving high highs, bullshit highs, not-caring, fuck-it highs. He wanted me to break me, the me I'd made, the me I'd needed to make, my need, mine, my whole life since I could remember. I didn't want to hear him that night. When I was ready to change I'd change. When life opens up before you, when you don't really know death and how quickly it can shorten the horizon, it's easy to promise yourself change. Keeping the lines hard, the parts of me separate, was what I knew, how I lived. I hadn't been ready to change. I hadn't been ready to listen. Paul pushed and I pushed back. Paul pushed and I ran. I ran and he was killed. Time is too slow and too fast and I want to fall, fall and not think, drink and not think, but I hear Mel's breathing, her quiet breathing, far away with Paul. I listen to her breathing and wait.

"I remember," she says, her voice still gone.

"Okay."

"Okay," she says and I wait.

"Okay," she says and her voice is almost sober. "Let's go back to that bar."

"Angel's Share."

"Angel's Share. We'll see if we can escape the world this time. It didn't work too well last time. But I think I can try to make it work this time. Maybe it's up to us. The trick is to remember and to escape at the same time."

"When are you free?"

"Always," Mel says. "I'm always free."

She laughs at the word and that makes it sadder.

"When would you like to meet?" I say.

"Friday. Let's meet Friday. Then I won't have to go to work the next day and you won't have to tell me anything about acting irresponsibly."

"I didn't tell you anything now."

"You're right. You didn't."

Outside my one window I can see a piece of sky. I hear the ice against glass, the sip.

"I almost want to go a little crazy. Just go crazy. Just let myself go. Will you be there if I do?" she says.

"Yes."

"Are you sure? Are you sure sure? A better me. A better you."

She laughs a small, closed laugh.

I swallow.

Her breathing is close to the phone now. "What's that line from *Hamlet* you used to say? The one about seems."

Paul and I met in a scene study class. HB Studios on Bank Street. I was taking the class to make it. Paul was taking the class for fun. After class we'd go to Chumley's, a famous speakeasy a few blocks away, and it was easy talking, easy laughing, easy drinking with him and when we drank we almost never talked acting and I think he knew, even then, I didn't love it.

"*Seems, madame. Nay, it is. I know not seems.*"

"That one. I knew it, but I wanted you to say it. He used to say it too."

"No seems. I'll be there."

"Don't worry," she says. "I haven't let myself go. I'm only drinking. But at least it sounds good. At least it sounds like you can protect me without any seems. He used to say that line too. *Seems, madame. Madame* is such an old-sounding word, but the way he said it, it sounded modern, like people called each other *madame* all the time."

"He was good."

"Your lines," she says.

"I'll see you Friday," she says.

And she hangs up like that.

The jet-fuel fire was 2000 degrees. A crematorium hits corpses with 1400 degrees.

After I ran to the towers, after I watched the towers burn, after one tower fell and then the other tower fell, I turned around and walked back in the direction of Father Demo Square where I'd been sitting. Everyone outside was looking south. There was nothing to see anymore, but they were looking. I walked past them. I walked past my street. I kept walking.

Downtown where I lived, close enough to the collapsed buildings to taste the bitter, burnt air against your tongue and gums, the living people all looked a little dead. There were no cars driving the streets except for a pick-up truck or van coming from downtown, ashy debris flying off hoods and fenders when the wind blew, people turning their sad faces to shield their eyes and mouths from the dust. We were breathing bodies. The streets were unnaturally quiet, broken by an occasional ambulance siren, pointless noise since there were no survivors. The other predominant sound was the voice of the 1010 WINS newscaster coming from car radios. Someone would be sitting in a parked car, the doors open, the radio turned up, people huddled around and listening to the news as if this attack had taken place somewhere else.

I kept walking. One radio blended into another radio, the congregation around each car standing with heads bent like at a funeral, and when a person left the circle of listeners the solemn face would remain solemn, the bent head would remain bent, a solitary fighter walking into the ring but without the robe, without the name emblazoned across the back, just a New Yorker in work clothes, walking forward, but really these walks looked direction-less except everyone, everyone, was walking uptown. The one other noise, popping every few minutes, was the sonic boom of the fighter jet above, air-splitting pops clarifying the potential for more attacks, which sent a thrill through me that this was it, this was war, but there was no joy like in the movies when the charge is called and the charge is made, when the implications of what can actually happen are forgotten in a collective scream of defiance.

There were already signs in the store windows offering water, use of the telephone, use of the bathroom, this hard city suddenly soft, this selfish city suddenly generous, this fast city suddenly slow, now that it was under attack. After the panic, after the fight or the flight, the heart slows. There were signs calling for blood, hospital addresses written in bold letters.

It was easy to spot the ones who'd been there. Debris still dusted their faces, a yellowish powder the color of flower pollen anointing them as survivors. It was easy to spot the ones who'd lost someone. Clutching cell phones, faces tear-streaked, mouths slack with resignation, then contorting to hopeless grimaces from cries caught in their throats. Next to one parked car with its radio on, a man screamed at the city, calling out anyone from Afghanistan, swearing to kill them all with his hands.

All the subways were down. All the buses were packed, driving up empty avenues, free to board but not worth getting on there were so many people waiting at each stop.

The farther uptown I walked, the more unreal the day became and the more faraway downtown felt. By the time I was on Fifth Avenue and Central Park, the air was fresh as city-air could get. There wasn't a trace of smoke or debris or tragedy. A few moody faces, but faces were often moody, no different from any other day. The only thing out of the ordinary was the single fighter jet circling overhead, flash of silver against blue backdrop. But the jet passed quickly. Then it was all calm on the uptown front.

I walked into a bar.

Chairs were pulled away from the tables and arranged like at some off-off Broadway theater where I'd done too many showcases, badly staged post-modern experiments that never received backers. This time I was a spectator. No stage, no actors, only the TV that kept showing the plane going into the South Tower, or the South Tower falling while the North Tower looked on, or the North Tower falling, a solitary crumble somehow more sad than terrifying. By that time the collapse seemed inevitable. One was down, the next would follow. The second tower going down, the North Tower, was harder for me. That was the tower hit first. That was the tower I'd run to. That was the tower I'd counted down the floors. Paul's tower.

We all sat there and watched TV. Strays from the street, heads tilted upward, watching. When the falling-tower images were replayed to saturation point, the news showed people chased by debris like from a bad disaster movie. Then the news showed longer shots of the smoke-filled gap in the city's horizon, a familiar mouth with two punched-in teeth.

I watched. I drank. The bartender's hand was heavier than any bartender's hand I'd ever seen, an extension of his heart, of all our hearts, and the bourbon went down, the heavy-handed pours becoming one long heavy-handed pour, and on TV the towers were resurrected, again and again, so they could fall, again and again, one long falling. Afterward, everyone said it looked like a movie. Everyone said the same things. Watching it live, watching flames melting steel, was unreal. Watching what I'd seen on TV, what had just happened a mile away, was unreal. I watched the buildings fall and fall and I got drunk. That's when I went to need-drinking. That's when I went to needing time to skip.

The drinks got me walking downtown again. The drinks got me to my apartment, up the stairs, over to the phone, fingers on the numbers. Phones were down all over the city, overloaded by every single call across America coming here, but I punched the numbers anyway. Again. And again. And again. It numbed me. The repetition. The busy signal holding off the conversation. I'd been close enough to the building to count down the floors from the top and close enough to know that my only friend's office was right there, right above the hole in the North Tower.

I dialed. My fingers against the numbers. Again and again.

There were three possibilities, three nightmare scenarios I replayed over and over in my own footage. He was sitting at his desk when a shadow passed along his window like a cloud, but the cloud didn't disappear and there was that sound, the jet-engine sound I'd heard while sitting in Father Demo Square twenty blocks uptown from him, only louder. It was too strange even from ground level to really register. He was 103 stories up, at eye-level, and the shadow that passed across his desk and stayed there made him look up and there it was, an airplane coming forward, straight forward. What a spectacular sight that must have been before impact.

Or the plane hit near him and the explosion burned him up immediately, so fast, I hoped, the nerve endings in his flesh never had time to register pain.

Or he survived the impact and waited at a window, jagged glass and then a straight drop, looking at the people and the cars so far down it didn't seem possible, and he needed to make a decision, a decision that all his other decisions had led to, the end of life's line. To jump or not to jump. Not a figurative abyss but a literal one with fire and smoke and sounds of agony and melting steel, heat burning his back, and the fresh air out there, a jump away, a final jump and the heat so hot it wasn't a decision at all.

I dialed. Again. And again. And I was about to hit the numbers again when it started to ring and I pushed down the puke in my throat and waited for a voice.

It wasn't Mel's voice. It was a broken man's voice. It was Paul's father. No, they hadn't heard from Paul. No, they hadn't heard from anyone in Paul's office. Yes, they would pass my prayers on to Mel. Then Paul's father started crying and then he stopped and apologized and said good-bye.

I'm meeting Mel at Angel's Share.

I've left my place too early, which I do a lot these days. I walk around Washington Square, passing time. There's a makeshift memorial in the center circle with notes and pictures and someone's lit a candle that the wind can't quite put out. Fall leaves scratch across the paved paths.

I walk east. A subway stops below and people start coming up the stairs and she's there. We're supposed to meet at the bar, but she's in front of me and I follow her, watch her, her perfect posture, her head straight. The men that pass look her over, the bold ones turning their heads like I've seen them do many times. If I walk into the bar and act like I'm surprised to see her there first, it will be a lie. Her grief's too pure. I can't see her eyes, but I already know they're far away.

"Mel."

Her name out loud stops me. She stops and turns to my voice.

"Hello," she says and her smile is sad and polite.

"We're both early."

"We are, but we're not there yet."

"Do you want to walk around for a while?"

"I want to drink," she says.

We walk to Angel's Share. Our bodies are close. Her arm brushes mine. The streets aren't crowded. I look into the windows of some bars and there's hardly anyone drinking and when I'm drunk everyone else looks drunk, but I'm not drunk so maybe nobody else is. Sometimes I still feel like a kid, like I'm the star and everyone else is an extra, but with Mel walking next to me I can't be the center of the world. I don't think she'll fall tonight, but if she does I have to be ready. She'll be the falling one. I'll be the catching one. And I think that makes her the star.

I open the door to Angel's Share and follow her in, up the stairs, through the restaurant, through the second-floor door, anonymous and secret-looking. The Asian bartender is methodically mixing a cocktail. We find two seats at the end of the bar where we always find two seats and I wait for Mel to sit before I do. The bartender comes over. Mel orders her usual Old Fashioned. I order bourbon. We watch the bartender go to work, mulling the fruit, pouring the alcohol, placing the glasses on beverage napkins, nodding for us, for himself, for the drinks.

"Cheers," Mel says and we touch glasses.

We drink quietly. The bar fills. We're both thinking about Paul. He never came here, but he might have liked it for a while before he got restless looking at the pretty people. Then he would have gone to a bar where the bartender's job was to simply pull taps and pour shots. He would have ordered a slow-poured Guinness and a cheeseburger, happy to get a buzz after a day of work.

"I had a drink at Chumley's the other night," Mel says. "Two nights ago or maybe it was three."

"I haven't been there since the night Paul met you."

"Why not?"

"I just haven't."

"Well. It looks the same. They still have sawdust on the floor and those great big Labradors. They looked even fatter than I remember. I wonder how much beer those dogs drink."

"They always looked like the happiest dogs in New York."

"They still look happy," Mel says.

Mel moves her stirrer, once around, twice around, and then places it on her beverage napkin.

"We went there sometimes," she says. "After we met."

"To drink with the dogs."

"Those dogs could drink us under the table."

"You're probably right."

"It became a firemen's bar," she says. "It was busier than ever the other night. There were firemen all over the place, most of them cleaned up in their dress uniforms. Three different firemen asked for my number."

"They're the new stars. They're the new heroes. Heroes are supposed to get the girl."

"One of them told me his ladder company was one of the first ones there."

"That did a lot of good."

"That's what I told him."

"And what did he say?"

"He still asked for my number."

"Of course."

"Before I left Chumley's, I did something Paul did to me when we met. I wanted to see if it felt at all like I remembered. I stood very still and I closed my eyes and I touched my eyelids. No one had ever done that to me before. He came up to me and he told me he was waiting for me and I remember I just said *Well* and he didn't say anything to that. He just stayed on my eyes. He had the steadiest eyes I'd ever seen. I told him he didn't have to wait anymore. And then he said it. *Stop.* He said it quiet and calm and the bar had been so noisy when he walked up to me, but I heard him say *Stop* and it was like the word had two syllables instead of one. It sounded like the word itself stopped. And I closed my eyes in the middle of the bar and he touched my eyelids."

I finish my bourbon. It's mostly melted ice.

"Has anyone ever done that to you?" she says.

"Never."

"Have you ever done that to anyone?"

"No."

"Were you watching us?"

"I saw him go over to you."

"You were probably talking to someone else by then."

I had watched him touch her eyelids. It had looked like a scene from a movie, but it wasn't. I had never touched eyelids or had my eyelids touched. My friend had fallen first.

"So that's what I did in Chumley's the other night."

"Did anyone see you?"

"I don't know. I didn't really notice. I'm sure I looked very strange, but I wouldn't have cared if they had. Maybe the dogs saw me."

"Happy dogs."

"Two syllables," she says. "I sometimes say it out loud, trying to mimic him, but it never comes out the right way."

She finishes her drink.

"What word do you say out loud?" she says.

"I don't say any words out loud."

"You should try. Even when it doesn't come out the same way. It makes me remember him."

"I remember him."

"I know you do," she says. "Tell me what happened that night you fought."

"You know what happened."

"Paul told me a little, but not much."

"We fought."

"You didn't hit each other. He was upset and told me that much, but then he stopped talking."

I finish my drink, wait for the bartender to finish mixing a colorful cocktail, ask for another round. He puts two fresh beverage napkins in front of us. We sit quietly and watch him work. The bartender nods for us, for himself, for the drinks and moves down the bar.

"Tell me what happened," she says.

I drink half my drink. I touch my stomach for me, to see how hard it feels, and it's hard. I make it harder like when I'm drunk, when I tell strangers to punch my stomach, punch me hard as they can. Mel's watching my eyes.

"We were in the Corner Bistro," I say. "We went in for a couple of beers and a couple of burgers. We were in the back corner booth, the one near the window, and the table had so many names carved into it our beer mugs didn't look steady. I remember thinking how sad that was. That people believed carving their names into a beat-up table would insure some kind of permanence."

"You thought that even then?"

"You're right. I don't know. Maybe I thought it later, after it happened. Maybe I thought it just now. Time's that fucked up these days."

"Go on."

"I was on the side of the table with my back to the wall so I could see everyone eating and drinking. But all he could see was me. He started telling me how close the two of you were and how he wanted that for me."

"What else?"

"He told me to open my eyes. He told me that everything I did in life was for a bullshit high. The drinking and the women and the going out all the time and how I should open my eyes and try something new. He told me that even acting wasn't enough for me, that I didn't really love it, that I didn't love anything. He said I wasn't really living and he wanted me to live."

"To live," Mel says, but the words, repeated, don't sound alive at all.

"Go on," she says.

"He told me my whole life was less than a life. I did my best James Dean for him, but he didn't stop. I wanted him to laugh it off. I wanted to laugh it off, but he didn't stop. He told me he'd seen the best part of me and I wasn't living the best part of me and I didn't want to hear it. I told him he sounded like some religious zealot who once converted has to convert everyone else. I told him I'd rather fuck a hundred strangers passionately than one woman for the rest of my life. He was pushing me so I pushed back. I know what he was telling me was for me, but it didn't matter. I felt like I was being pushed and I pushed back hard and hateful and I couldn't stop. I told him he'd get tired of you and bored. I told him he was weak jumping in the way he'd jumped in. And I didn't stop there. I told him he'd get sick of fucking you and then we'd see how much he was living. He looked me right in the eyes. It was the first time I ever saw him angry. He was looking right in my eyes and he told me I was a little man."

I drink down the rest of my drink.

"I told him I should hit him."

Mel's eyes are blue and calm and she's looking at me like I'm the only one in the world, but behind her eyes I know she's seeing Paul.

"I told him I should hit him and he told me he'd never seen me hit anybody. I told him to fuck off and he said I was a scared little man. And maybe he was right. Maybe I was scared. Maybe I was scared to stop living the way I lived, but at that moment he wasn't talking about that. He was calling me scared in the way no man wants to be called scared. I wanted to hit him. I wanted to hurt him. I wanted to hit him as hard as I could in his face. But I didn't. I should have. If I'd hit him maybe it would have been over right there. He knew what I was thinking. He told me to try it. He told me to be as tough as I pretended for all those bullshit movie moments I was auditioning for. He leaned forward, looking right in my eyes and he told me to try it. He told me to be a man. I felt my gut turn over. He was right and I felt my gut turn over and it was like he felt it too, and he knew it, knew he'd won the fight before it even started, and then his eyes went from angry to kind. He wanted the best for me, but he should never have questioned me like that. I never questioned his life and he shouldn't have questioned mine. I hated him for questioning me and I didn't care how kind his eyes went or how steady his eyes were on mine. I moved my eyes. I moved my eyes and got up and left the bar and the only words in my head were *little man*. All the time we spent together and that's all I remembered."

My hands are fists. I open them. I lift my glass, but there's nothing left.

"I know you remember other things."

"That was the last thing."

"You would have spoken eventually," she says.

"But I didn't. And now I can't."

"There are a lot of things we both can't do."

"He should have waited for me to change. He was putting me against a wall when he questioned me. He should have waited."

"He wanted you to stop wasting time."

"I wasn't thinking about time then. Not like now."

"Nobody was," Mel says.

She sits very still, waiting for me to go on, showing me, maybe, that Paul could have waited too, just like this, but that he didn't wait for a reason, didn't wait because some waiting can last too long.

"It was my time to waste," I say. "Me looking at me, pretending I was the center of the world, playing my parts. Doing my best James Dean even if I didn't know anything about him except some pictures I'd seen in a book of old stars. I needed to pretend when I was a kid. Maybe I was too old to blame my past, but I'd needed to pretend. Paul was the only one I ever told. I told him all of it a few months after we met. Just once, but I told him all of it. I knew he'd remember. It was me in front of the mirror, me talking to me because no one else was around to listen. I told him all of it and he still called me a little man. It felt like a betrayal."

"He was questioning you. You questioned him."

"He put me against a wall."

"Do you still need to look in the mirror and pretend you're the star?" she says.

"I don't know."

"Maybe he sensed that. Maybe he sensed it was the right time to talk with you."

"Look at me," I say like a joke, but it's not.

Mel waits. She doesn't push. She doesn't even move her hand to her glass, move the glass to her lips.

"I'm still angry," I say, but her eyes have pushed off some of my anger. "I'm still angry at him and I'm still angry at me. I shouldn't have run away. I should have called him. I should have seen him. When the anger turns to sadness it's worse. That's worse. When I'm angry I don't miss him as much."

The bartender is mixing a complicated cocktail. I need another drink, a simple pour, a straight pour, a heavy-handed one and two and three and.

"Tell me," she says. "If he had died, if he had just died, would you be so angry?"

"He didn't just die."

"No," she says. "He didn't."

"And I don't know what to hit."

"And it makes you crazy."

I don't say anything.

"It makes me crazy too," she says.

The bartender comes over, clears our glasses and I nod my head for him. He pours us two more drinks, places them on two fresh napkins.

"*Devastare*," she says. That's the word that keeps coming to me. I took Latin all four years of high school and we had to translate so many sentences with that word. *Devastare*. To lay waste. It was always about fields, the Romans were always laying waste to people's fields, and it never sounded so bad to me, the word *devastare*, not as bad as devastate. Whenever the Romans were laying waste to something, I pictured these long fields being plowed under and that was all."

"*Devastare*."

"See? It doesn't sound so bad. They should use that word instead of devastate, instead of devastation. The news keeps using that word over and over again and it's an awful-sounding word. It's a word that has nothing to do with fields."

"How do you say field in Latin?"

"*Ager*. And farmer is *Agricola*. I liked that word too. Whenever someone mentioned Latin, if it happened to come up, Paul would say, *Bonum est libros legere. It is good to read books.* The phrase never had anything to do with the conversation, but he would say the words very earnestly and nod his head like he was thinking profound thoughts and everyone assumed he was a Latin scholar. Then he would smile at me when no one was looking. He was always entertaining me. *Bonum est libros legere.* It was the only Latin phrase he knew, the only one beside *in vino veritas,* and after he said it he'd smile for me and no one knew."

"When we visited Europe, the first question he asked in every country was how to say *I speak your language fluently, but I prefer to speak English.* I only remember the German one. *Ich spreche fliessend Deutsch.* He'd grab someone as soon as we got off the train and practice with them until he got the accent exactly right, until he sounded like he'd been born and bred wherever we were."

"I'm sure they enjoyed practicing with him."

"They did."

I finish my drink.

"It was never work," she says. "He made it so it never felt like work. I kept thinking something would change and become cold the way it was cold when I was growing up, but it didn't. When I met Paul it was like a thaw. I knew the cold was part of me, but after I met him I realized how much because it went away. Almost all of it went away."

She lifts her drink, drinks, puts her glass down.

"I know it was work for you when you fought," she says. "He was devastated after you fought. I should say *devastare,* right? We should think about fields instead. That's a nicer picture."

"*Devastare.*"

"I remembered just now. I never told Paul how I preferred that word."

"He already had his Latin phrase."

"I try to remember everything, every thing, but sometimes I forget something, I don't even know what it is sometimes, but I know it's not coming to me, something about him isn't coming to me and when that happens, when a piece is missing, it makes me crazy. I don't know what to do with that. So I think about him and I say his words out loud and I touch my eyelids like some crazy woman in the middle of a bar, but that's not the crazy part. The crazy part is if I forget."

"You won't forget."

"Are you sure?"

"No one ever touched your eyelids before. It's not a place people touch. So you won't forget."

She closes her eyes for a moment and then opens them.

"Stop," she says.

She lets the word stay there.

"That's almost how he said it, but not quite. It's missing something when I say it. When he said it, it was like the word had two syllables."

She lifts her drink and drinks, drinks it down. Mine is already down. I lift my drink, take an ice cube in my mouth, bite, swallow.

One July afternoon Paul and I were playing softball in Central Park. We weren't part of a team, but on the weekends teams sometimes needed extra players and so we played catch along the sidelines, showing off our strong arms until we got into a game. I liked the outfield where I could run around the grass. Paul liked playing third base, falling to his knees, his body a wall without holes, pulling in ripped balls and throwing runners out. When we happened to be on the same team, Paul at third and me in left, I didn't have to move if the batter hit a line drive or lower. Paul fielded everything, even bad hops, willing to take one on the chest for the team that wasn't his.

The humidity had been building all day, making the pavement soft and holding the exhaust close to the street. A few innings into the game horizontal lighting cracked over Harlem. The clouds moved closer and when a bolt snapped from one side of the park to the other, the home plate umpire called the game. The players scattered. Paul and I jogged out of Central Park to Columbus Circle and the first drops started to fall. People ran under awnings, into stores.

The drops came heavier and I ran for cover, but Paul called me back. He took off his shirt, looked at the sky and waited.

"The only thing to worry about is the lightning," he yelled and started laughing, a cut of dimple in his right cheek. He had an easy laugh.

"You're going to get soaked in a minute."

"I need a shower." He was yelling over the rain. "Take off your shirt. It feels great. The rain feels great if you just let it. And there's as much chance of us getting struck by lightning as there is of us getting struck by lightning."

It was solid logic and more, the kind of freedom that only comes when some danger is involved, when you test mortality just enough to feel the preciousness of life, to feel the high that life can sometimes be. So I took off my shirt.

We stood there bare-chested as the darkest clouds moved over us. I watched the lightning, counted down to the thunder, a sound-travel trick I'd learned as a kid. The bolts came closer and closer and then one landed right in front of us, cracked off a hydrant, so close the thunder vibrated against our feet. Paul was yelling a gut-pitched yell full of life and I realized I was doing the same.

The summer before we'd traveled to Europe together. In Pamplona we saw the running of the bulls. We didn't run, too happily hungover like most Pamplona revelers, but the first morning of the festival we went to the bullring to watch. The sun was already hot and we each held a bottle of sweet Sangria, a perfect breakfast drink. We heard the firecracker that signaled the start of the run and a few minutes later the runners crammed through the bullring's small entrance, their faces frantic and then more frantic until the bulls ran in, horns at the ready. The runners spread out in the bullring, the bulls stopped and looked around, not sure what to do, and then the oxen patiently herded the bulls across the ring and out of sight. I studied the human faces.

The people who'd run, the people who'd run close enough to touch the bulls, were ecstatic. They'd felt the high of life because for a moment they'd put their lives in danger.

"We should have run."

"Why?" Paul said.

"To say we ran."

"It means nothing to us. I don't understand the ritual of bullfights and I definitely don't understand the ritual of this run."

"People are going to ask why we didn't run when they find out we were in Pamplona."

"Let them. I used to work with a guy who came here every summer to run with the bulls. He ran so close he'd get his picture in the morning papers and he plastered those pictures all over his office. Every time he could, no matter what anyone was talking about, he'd figure out a way to bring up Pamplona. Sometimes I'd tell him I had reservations at a Spanish restaurant just to see him work the conversation back to the bulls. It was almost fascinating. Then I stopped. I started to feel sorry for him. His whole identity was wrapped into his once-a-year run."

"What's our identity wrapped into?"

"Hopefully not what we do to impress people."

"I want to impress people."

Paul tipped his bottle of sangria, then wiped his hand across his mouth and smiled. "You impress me."

"I want to make my mark."

"Then make your mark."

"My mark depends on other people being impressed."

"Are you trying to impress anyone right now?"

"No one's here who can help me."

"How does it feel?"

"I'm not thinking about it."

"Exactly. There's no reason to strut your stuff. We're living life, traveling around. We don't even need to run with the bulls. There's nothing to prove here. There's no one watching us and even if there were, who cares?"

"I need to be watched. I'm trying to make it. That's what I do."

"You're not being watched all the time."

"I have to be ready."

Paul put his hands over his eyes. He was hair, forehead, hands, smile.

"Good," I said. "Keep your hands there."

He kept his hands there. "See?"

"You can't see."

"I can't see you," he said. "You should try not to see you so much. That's the great thing about traveling. It gets you outside yourself and there's something pure about that. Even when I'm not traveling, I try to remember how it feels when I am."

"Pure." It was like a word I'd never heard before.

"Pure like those bulls running. They're just running."

"They're animals."

Paul lifted his hands from his eyes. "If you're too aware of everything, you can't move."

"I can move."

"There's a difference between moving and posing. I'd rather be the bull than those runners trying to get their faces in the papers."

"What about the runners running to run."

"I'd rather be them," Paul said.

"Then why are we sitting here?"

"We're sitting. We're drinking. We're talking. We're here. That's enough."

He put his arm around me. "I'd rather be us."

The rest of the trip, I tried to strut less, look around more, get outside myself.

Columbus Circle. Me and Paul with our shirts off, facing the sky, no one watching, the rain so heavy, so hard, it did feel great if you let it and the lightning hit and we yelled.

Taking a subway away from a woman's apartment. Drinking a Yoo-hoo to soothe my throat. Eating a burger to soak some alcohol. Getting to my place, my bed. The sparrows coming out right when I close my eyes, their optimism about a new day rotten in my ears. Sleeping. Waking. Running a hungover run. Taking the subway to the Art Students League. Standing. The sound of charcoal touching paper. Going home. Getting in bed. Sun patterns on the floor.

I dream a World Trade Center dream. I'm walking

through a paved-over lot, a gigantic, empty, flat space absurdly big for a city. At the end of the lot there's a towering building, over one hundred stories high. I'm almost at the building when I see the plane flying low. I turn and start to run. I run but can't run fast enough. I hear the crash and I'm still running when the heat from the explosion hits my back. I see the explosion even with my back turned and the heat gets hotter and the light's too light. It's my third World Trade Center dream. The third I can remember.

I'm meeting Mel at Angel's Share.

I shower, dress. Check myself in the mirror. And then I say his name quietly the way she must say his name. *Paul*. And then I say her name quietly. *Mel*.

I turn off the lights, walk out the door.

The city's Friday-night busy. I stop at the newsstand to buy a pack of Big Red where the Arab man never says thank you. Before September 11th I didn't care, but now I do. Most Arabs in this city have become contrite. Middle Eastern taxi drivers paste American flags to their cab windows. Photographs of the twin towers hang in Arab-owned falafel stands. Most Arabs walk the streets with eyes averted, looking down in shame, or at least pretend-shame. But this man at the newsstand hasn't changed at all. I've started holding the quarter between my thumb and index finger until he's forced to snatch it from me like some third-world beggar. I watch his eyes the whole time. He could stay on my eyes, try to win the eye-game, but it's his job to collect change for packs of gum and candy and newspapers and he needs his eyes to get the quarter from my fingers. He chooses to lose every time. As soon as the quarter is his, he looks at my eyes to see me looking at him, me, a fair-haired, light-eyed American.

I walk through Washington Square, past the dog run where the dogs are running wild within the confines of the fence. The dog owners stand around talking, some smoking, lit tobacco like fireflies on this cold night. But the dogs don't care. They're with their own and being with their own takes all their focus. I stop to watch the dogs. There's a dog fucking in the dog run, moving in and out, in and out, his head turning left and right, looking for the next bitch to mount and if he lost a dog friend he's not thinking about that friend now.

The rest of the park is quiet. A dealer asks if I want some smoke. Business is back to business.

I rub my hands together. I haven't bought new gloves yet. The cold nights are lining up consistently now.

I walk east, walk through the front door, walk up the stairs, through the restaurant, through the unmarked door. Two bartenders are working, their methodical movements practically synchronized, mulling fruit, squeezing lemons, pouring alcohol, nodding for the drinks when they place them on beverage napkins. She's at the end of the bar.

Mel is drinking. But drinking, part of her fall, part of my fall, isn't enough. Falling. That's how I picture it. It's the fall after the first grief and after the slow sadness and after the dead feeling. I know it can happen, not a vague, easy, time-heals cliché, but a moment as real as the loss, that you can point to and say this is when life started again. Mel's drinking, she's holding on, beyond the crying that I also picture, the crying she must do late at night, or worse, in the morning when the sun is out and the whole day to get through is before her. But she hasn't fallen yet. I picture the fall and it's not unlike the fall of all those bodies that day. It starts horribly, those first moments through air unattached to anything, but then the speed must slow, not the real speed but the feeling of speed, seconds and seconds of falling and not hitting anything, and the hands and feet, the arms and legs, even the heart must move from clenched fear to something else, to letting go, to acceptance. I can't picture the end of the fall. It's not like the concrete they hit. You start life again, you go on, but not like before. It's only close to before. That part is vague. It's close to before. But at least you go on. And that's what I hope for. For her. For me.

I picture the catch differently. I couldn't catch a body falling that far. No one caught bodies that day. I picture the catch like I'm in the outfield. The ball is hit and you have to judge it, from the sound and the height and the speed, judge it just right and then wait. Sometimes the ball's so high the wait feels too long, but eventually it reaches that point where it can't go any higher and it starts to fall. You're watching it, judging it, glove open, waiting to take it in. I don't know how she'll fall or when she'll fall. But I have to hold on and wait, hold on and catch, hold on and take her in, and then she'll go on.

I walk to Mel. There's an Old Fashioned in front of her, and in her eyes it's easy to see she's had more than one drink. She smiles when she sees me. A full smile and not just the beginning of a smile. She takes a long sip right before I get to her.

"I beat you," she says.

She kisses my cheek and I kiss hers.

"How long have you been here?"

"Not so long," she says. "You look like you've been in the sun."

"It's the cold."

"Did you run this morning?"

"I ran."

"Even in the cold. Even though you were out late. You were out late, weren't you? I can see it. I know what that looks like, you know."

"How was work?"

"I didn't feel like going in today, so I didn't. They understand less and less. My calling in sick is no longer a good enough euphemism for grieving, but they're still too awkward to say anything. Eventually they'll let me go."

"Do you want them to let you go?"

"Do you want to keep running?"

"I don't know if I want to. But I'm running anyway."

"I don't know if I want to work."

"That's the feeling these days."

"These days. These days. When will these days end?"

The way she asks, half sad, half a test, sounds like she's

picking up where Paul left off. Like there was a skip between the last time, when I ran from him, too many questions, and now.

My hands are fists.

"What are you drinking?" she says. "The usual?"

"That's why it's the usual," I say.

A man stands near us waiting for his own drink. He smiles at Mel. She nods her head like an Angel's Share bartender who's finished concocting a cocktail. The man picks up his drink and moves. I get the real bartender's attention and order a bourbon rocks, count the alcohol going in.

"I saw the strangest thing today," Mel says. "I was taking a walk uptown and right in front of me, crossing the street, was a man in a leather mask with a dog collar around his neck. A woman was walking him on a leash. She was dressed in heels and a fur coat and sunglasses that hid her eyes. I would have liked to have seen her eyes. She even told the man in the dog collar where the curb was so he wouldn't fall. I've never seen that in the city before. And no one even flinched. A few people laughed, but most people just looked and then looked away. I guess we've seen everything in this city. Nothing's surprising anymore."

"A man walker."

"She must be making a fortune. I don't think they ever sleep with the men that pay them. They just walk them around or order them around. It would take the mystery and the power away if they ever slept with the men, so they keep them on a leash."

"Where was this?"

"Above 86th Street, I think. I'm not sure exactly how far up. How's your bourbon? Did Li pour you a long enough count?"

"Li?"

"The bartender."

"A first-name basis with the bartender. You've been frequenting this place."

"Only with very special people," she says and laughs. "Only with people who can keep a secret."

"Good. We don't want the masses taking over Angel's Share."

"They found three bodies today," Mel says.

"I heard on the news."

"It wasn't Paul. I think they'd have called me already. They must call people before they announce it on the news. Every time the phone rang today I picked up before the first ring ended, but it was never them."

"They'll keep digging as long as the weather's good."

"It's been great weather for digging, hasn't it?"

Mel orders another drink, calling Li by name, saying she'll have another. She knows Li's name. Li knows her drink.

"I never thought I'd say that sentence," Mel says. "It's been great weather for digging. It's a nice day to dig. A nice day to dig. That sounds like a title. Or a line for an ad campaign."

Mel takes a long sip of her Old Fashioned. Her eyes are

lighter than ever, lighter than I remember, the kind of pale blue I'd expect on a blind person, as if her eyes had been flipped, the bluest part looking inside and the lightest blue facing out for the world to see, but not for her to see the world. Mel spears a piece of mulled fruit with her stir stick and chews. Her face is gaunt, like all she's been eating is fruit saturated with whiskey.

"Why don't we get some dinner?"

"I'm not hungry," she says.

"I could go for a steak. What do you say we go to the Strip House?"

"You don't have to take me to the Strip House. If I were hungry I'd be happy with a cheeseburger."

"Let's spend some money. What the hell? I just got a part in a big-budget film."

"Really?"

"No."

"Have you been auditioning?"

"Not these days."

I look around the bar. It's dark out so the windows that look out on the street reflect what's inside, not outside. The long bar. The people drinking, a little blurry in the reflection. Me and Mel.

"Friday night," Mel says.

I look away from the window. The faces look clearer but not that clear, like the low light and alcohol have smeared their features.

"Did you work today?" she says.

"I stood for three classes. When the next Michelangelo comes to town, I'll be in shape to stand for weeks. Weeks and weeks. I'll be ready to be the next David."

"You're already David."

"Look at me. Larger than life. Not a little man at all."

"Don't," she says. "Don't. Let's just drink. Let's just drink Li's drinks at Angel's Share and escape from the world. So what were we talking about?"

"Food."

"Yes. Food. Next time I'm really hungry I'll take you to a steak house. I should be getting a chunk of money soon. Hopefully the bigwigs at Cantor Fitzgerald will pay up before the guilt subsides. Until that happens I better not quit my day job. I better attend my day job."

She lifts her glass.

"To day jobs," she says and laughs.

"Cheers," she says and finishes her drink.

I unclench my fist.

"He actually came," Mel says.

Her eyes are staring across the room.

"Bill Junkins," Mel says. "I told him where I was going, but I told him not to come. It was sort of a test."

I turn, follow where her pale eyes are looking. I see a man I vaguely recognize. He's tall and in shape, dressed in a suit and silk tie. He looks rich. He looks like a central-casting rich man. Plain, handsome features, uninteresting enough to make it to the top of the company ladder without a hitch. His face on the cover of a business magazine or an annual financial report would say stability, prudence, hard work, corporate America.

"It's very flattering, but very pitiful. He's a prick, a prick to everyone else, but with me he's like a high school kid."

"The high school kid most likely to succeed."

"He's certainly succeeded."

The man's suit and tie look out of place in this room. He stops in front of Mel.

"What a coincidence," Mel says.

"I thought I'd come by for a quick drink."

"So you did."

"I was in the neighborhood. I was at a function."

"A function."

"For charity."

Mel tilts her glass, the mulled fruit still at the bottom

"Junkins, this is my friend, David."

"Bill," he says and shakes my hand. "You look familiar. Have we met before?"

"He should look familiar," Mel says. "He's sort of famous."

"Is he?"

"He's in galleries all over the city."

"I don't see as much art as I'd like."

"Nobody does," I say.

"You met David at a party," Mel says.

Junkins nods his head at me but not like the bartenders. I look past him, at the fresh beverage napkins, at the drinks, at the bartenders working, at the people having fun on Friday night.

"Junkins used to work with Paul," Mel says.

"Back in my Cantor days," Junkins says.

"Your Cantor days." Mel tilts her glass again. "Is that how you refer to them?"

Bill Junkins sort of smiles, his mouth stuck.

"Got out just in time, didn't you, Junk?" Mel says. "Got out of Cantor just in time. Talk about impeccable timing. Almost like tonight. Almost like having a charitable function in the neighborhood."

Bill Junkins' mouth stays in an uncomfortable twist. His eyes are angry, but he's trying to keep the smile in them and I place the name with the riled face. I remember the story Paul told. There was a new temp at the office and Bill Junkins asked him to go down and get him a sandwich for lunch. The temp balked at the request. He said he wasn't a delivery boy, said he was hired to do office work, not fetch lunches. Bill Junkins slapped the temp across the face, hard enough to dislocate the man's jaw. To keep the firm's name out of the papers, Cantor Fitzgerald paid the temp some serious money.

Mel lifts her empty glass.

"I'm ready," she says to Bill Junkins.

He leans into the bar and the bartender comes over. Mel orders another Old Fashioned, a bourbon for me and a Gibson, three onions, for Junkins.

"Three onions, right, Junk?"

"Thank you," he says.

I watch the bartender make the drinks, place them on three fresh beverage napkins, nod three times. Bill Junkins hands the bartender his credit card.

"Cheers," Mel says and starts on her drink.

Bill Junkins watches her.

"How many have you had?" he says.

"I'm not counting."

"I think you're drunk."

"Do you?"

He doesn't say anything, his mouth a straight-lined frown.

"Am I slurring my words?" she says.

"No."

"Would you like me to walk a straight line?"

"That's not necessary."

"Are you afraid I'll embarrass you? I can walk a straight line right now if you like. I can walk a straight line right through the crowd and a straight line right out of here."

"What if the straight line led you downtown?"

"That's not nice," Mel says.

"I'm sorry."

"It's not nice to hit below the belt. It's like slapping, Junk. You can get in a great deal of trouble for slapping."

Bill Junkins' face flushes.

"You're looking to get a rise out of me," he says.

"You can leave whenever you want."

Mel still doesn't walk downtown. She walks east and

west and uptown but never downtown. When she goes downtown she takes the subway past where she has to go so she can walk uptown, so she doesn't have to look. Bill Junkins doesn't seem like a walker. I see company cars. I see late-night cabs. She must have confided her walking patterns when they were drinking together. They must have been drinking together, maybe here, this place where you should bring special people, or people you pretend are special, this place where you can say all kinds of things you'll forget.

"All I said was that I thought you'd been drinking," Bill Junkins says.

"No. You said you thought I was drunk. Did you think I'd be drunk when you decided to come here?"

"I wasn't sure."

"But you came anyway."

"I was a few blocks away," he says, as much for me as for Mel.

Mel's eyes move away from us and she looks around the bar. It's easy to see Bill Junkins hates this, her looking around, and it's easy to see Mel knows he hates this. The way she once looked around was natural, but now she's putting on a show. I know about look-at-me eye games. I know about wanting to be watched. Mel's posing. Another entry on the list of damages since that day.

"Do you live in this neighborhood?" Junkins says to me.

"Close enough."

"I assume a lot of artists do."

"Artists and people who pretend they're artists. This

city's full of those."

"I'm sure," Junkins says and pretends to survey the room. Acting everywhere.

"Can you find the real one?" I say.

"The real what?"

"Can you find the real artist out of all these fakes drinking their drinks?"

"That sounds like a fun game," Mel says.

"So let's play it," I say.

"Don't," Mel says.

"Start at the other end of the bar," I say. "Or we can start at this end. At my end."

"Are you a fake?" Junkins says.

"I'm not an artist. I just stand."

"You stand?"

"He works as an artist's model," Mel says. "And he's an actor too."

"Hey diddle dee dee," I say.

"Are you really?" Junkins says.

"Am I really what? These days I'm a drinker."

I finish my drink and put the glass on the bar.

"An artist's model," Junkins says. "So you stand there naked?"

"I stand there naked."

"Don't you feel strange doing that?"

"Do you feel strange in the shower?"

"I'm alone in the shower."

"It's not that different when you're thinking about other

things."

"You must have to stand very still," Junkins says.

"That's not strange either. Especially when you don't feel like moving."

"You never feel like moving?"

"I can stand at a bar all night and not move."

"As long as the drinks keep coming," Junkins says and smiles, but I'm not smiling.

He puts his fingers in the gin, picks out an onion and puts it in his mouth. "This is the most crowded I've seen this place," he says.

"It's Friday night," Mel says. "Isn't it?"

"I thought the weekend would never come. We had a crazy week at work."

"I'm going to call it a night," I say.

"Don't go," Mel says.

"I'm tired."

"You just got here. You don't look tired. He doesn't look tired, does he, Junk?"

"I don't know him," Junkins says. "I'm not enrolled in any art classes."

There's a smirk in his voice, but I leave it alone.

"Of course you're not," Mel says. "You're on the other side of the world."

"Not completely," he says. "Making money is creative."

"Then you must be a very creative man."

"I am a very creative man."

"Let's start with you then," she says. "Fake artist or real

artist?"

"I don't pretend to be an artist."

"You just pretend to be interesting. You pretend people are interested in you for more than your money."

Junkins shakes his head. "I'm going to keep my mouth shut."

"What an interesting comeback."

"You're drunk. I have an unfair advantage."

"Do you think you could win with a fair advantage?"

Junkins' eyes go narrow.

"Don't look so angry, Junk. You used to have a sense of humor when you worked at Cantor."

"Nice to meet you again," I say. "I'll talk to you later, Mel."

"Don't go yet. You can go wash your face. You'll wake up."

She takes my wrist in her hand and she's looking at me, not playing-games looking, at least I don't think so.

"Please," she says.

"I'm tired."

"Please. We'll have another drink."

"I don't need another drink."

"We all need another drink," she says.

I want to leave. She wants me to stay. I want to drink alone. She wants to drink with company. I have to catch her when she falls.

"Let's drink," Junkins says.

"You have a toast to make?" I say.

Junkins looks away.

"Is there someone you'd like to drink to?" I say.

He's pretending to survey the polished bottles behind the bar.

"Stay," Mel says.

"Cheers."

"Please stay," she says.

"Let me wash my face."

I walk to the bathroom. I press cold water into my eyes. I blink. Blink again. I'm looking at myself in the mirror. Look at me. Look at her. I punch the mirror. The mirror doesn't break. My face is still there. My knuckles swell. I can move my fingers so nothing's broken.

I walk back. Mel's talking to Junkins and he's standing too straight, too conspicuous. Then he points his finger at her and she laughs. I can hear her laugh under the crowd's noise and the music. I get closer and her eyes pick me up and stay on me until I'm next to her.

"Feel better?"

"Much."

"Would you like another drink?" Junkins asks. "I've started a tab."

"I think I'm done drinking for the night."

"That's not like you," Mel says.

"This is quite a place," Junkins says.

"I like it," I say.

"I like it too. Don't get me wrong."

"I'm not getting you wrong."

"You're a bourbon drinker, right? I was at Le Cirque for lunch and they have a great selection of bourbons. Have you ever been?"

"Never."

Mel takes my wrist for the second time tonight and looks at my hand.

"What did you do in there?"

"I didn't do anything."

"What did you do in there?"

"Nothing."

Mel moves her fingers over my raised knuckles. "Does it hurt?"

"No."

"Do you see that, Junkins?" she says, but she doesn't care whether he sees it or not. She's holding my wrist and Junkins could be all the way uptown for all she cares. The bar feels far away, blurred bodies and faces and only her hand on my wrist is clear and the pain in my knuckles.

"I want to hit things too," she says. "I'll be drinking in my kitchen and all of a sudden I'm throwing the glass against the wall. It doesn't help, but it's what you said. It's better than sadness. The sadness just stays there heavy and lazy and tired and I don't have the energy to throw any-thing."

She lets go of my wrist. She finishes her drink. Her eyes go far away, turn lighter than light, then come back.

"That's good luck somewhere, isn't it?" Mel says. "Break-ing glasses. In what country is that good luck? I think it's

Greece. Is it Greece, Junk?"

"I don't know."

"It's definitely good luck somewhere."

The bartender comes over.

"I'll have another drink, Li," she says.

"Why don't you wait a while?" Junkins says.

"Because I don't believe in waiting these days."

"You're drinking too much."

"Not too much."

"It doesn't look good on you."

"Then why are all the men looking at me?"

"Men like to look."

"The difference is I look back now. I look back the way I used to. I look them right in their lecherous eyes until they get uncomfortable. Most of them don't know what to do. Can you hold my eyes, Junk?"

"I'm not going to play this game with you."

"But you are. You're playing it right now."

Junkins looks away.

"Do you ever break things, Junk?"

Mel laughs. Her mouth wide and open. I can see all the way to the back of her throat.

"Do you?" Mel says. "Just for the hell of it? Just all of a sudden?"

"I'm going to go," I say.

"Have one more."

"I don't feel like it."

"That's not like you, David."

"It's like me now."

"Okay," she says, her mouth so relaxed, almost a smile, but not. "Okay. I understand."

"I am a little drunk," she says.

"More than a little," Junkins says.

"You counting?" I say.

Junkins moves his eyes.

"He's a numbers man," Mel says. "He doesn't like to calculate why. He likes to calculate how much."

"I'm sorry," he says.

"Don't be. It's not your fault you weren't there."

"I don't feel guilty about that."

"You shouldn't. You made the smart move when you moved."

"It wouldn't have looked good to stay in the same building after I started my own firm. They bombed the place once, you know. People forget about that."

"Tell Junk that Shakespeare quote," Mel says to me. "One of the ones you and Paul used to say."

"*The lady doth protest too much, methinks.*"

"That's the one. You like Shakespeare, Junk?"

"I only read him when I had to in college."

"*The lady doth protest too much, methinks,*" Mel says.

"What are you saying? Are you saying I'm a coward?" Junkins says.

"Have a sense of humor, Junk. But please don't tell me how much I should or shouldn't drink. No matter how much I drink I won't forget the reason I'm drinking."

Mel takes my wrist for a third time, looks at my swollen knuckles, then lets go.

"What do you want to do, Junkins?" she says.

"Whatever you want."

"You hate it when I call you Junkins, don't you?"

"I prefer Bill."

"You hate it when I call you Junk."

Junkins doesn't say anything.

"What about William?" she says. "Like William Shakespeare."

"William is fine."

"What about Billy? Is Billy too informal?"

He's actually taking her shit. He's actually standing there, holding it in, keeping his temper in check and taking her shit.

"I have to go," I say.

"Nice to meet you again," he says.

He puts out his hand so I put out mine and the pain shoots from my knuckles into my wrist. He's gripping me hard to let me know he's still a man. I could take out my cock and show it to him, like I'm standing in front of the room, hands moving charcoal over paper, but I don't. There are already too many games in this bar.

"You're sure you can't stay for one more drink?" Mel says.

"I have to go."

"He must have a date," Mel says to Junkins. "David always has a date."

"Good night, Mel."

Her eyes are on my eyes and for a moment I feel like the only person in the world. She moves her head to me. Her lips touch my cheek. Her mouth is alcohol-warm. I could take her head in my hand, bring her lips to my lips, take her out of here. But I don't.

I watch her lips change to a smile, a smile I don't recognize, and her eyes move to Junkins.

"I'll have another Old Fashioned, Bill. I like watching Li work. He knows exactly the right ratio of bitters to sugar."

Junkins leans into the bar.

"Angel's Share," she says. "It's the perfect name for this place, don't you think?"

"I guess," Junkins says.

"No. It is. It's perfect."

I run.

Big-screen TVs all over the place and the baseball game is on. New York should win if you're fool enough to believe such things. If there's any optimistic symbolism in the world, the Yankees should take this year's World Series once again. But on all the big screens, a visual crescendo of repetitions, one out multiplied into many outs, the Yankees are losing. They're not only losing, they're losing so bad it's clear they're overmatched and it's clear to me that symbolism will, to use the baseball cliché, go down swinging. I can already imagine the press conferences, the easy apho-risms, the positive spins, delivered by ballplayers in all their homogenized glory. Of course, it's only baseball. New York needs more than a World Series to ease its loss.

"To John," Garrett says and the three of us, me, Garrett, and a friend Garrett brought along, touch plastic cups.

We've been drinking bourbon and Cokes. We've been talking about John, who went to law school with Garrett and his friend.

John worked as a lawyer for the police department. He happened to be at a downtown precinct when the first plane hit, so he threw on a police shirt and ran toward the fire with the other officers. He was helping people coming down the stairs.

"He was a funny guy," Garrett says. "Definitely not the typical law school student. He always seemed a little lost, but in a good way, like there was more to life than passing the Bar. I walked by a hardware store yesterday and I saw his face in the window. They made his picture into a poster and at the bottom it said *Johnny I hardly knew ya* like that famous war song. I guess he was a regular customer. I didn't even know he was dead."

"*Johnny I hardly knew ya,*" I say.

"I still can't believe it," Garrett says. "I'm about ready to join the military. I'm about ready to enlist."

"And do what?" Garrett's friend says.

"And fight. If I knew I could go to war over there and not get killed, I'd drop everything and enlist right now."

"Brave man," Garrett's friend says.

"Hollywood," I say.

"That's your dream," Garrett says. "My dream is to enlist and kick some Taliban ass."

"But not get hurt."

"At least not badly."

"That's Hollywood."

"I'm just saying," Garrett says. "I'm just saying what I'd like to do."

"Joining the military isn't going to bring John back," Garrett's friend says.

"I didn't even know he was dead until I saw his picture."

"Three thousand," Garrett's friend says. "Three thousand dead or missing. What a waste."

I wonder what the September 11th math would show. Three thousand dead or missing multiplied by however many potential years of life.

"David lost his best friend," Garrett says.

"I'm sorry," Garrett's friend says.

Derek Jeter strikes out, a televised echo of bat missing ball.

I finish my drink and go to the bar. I'm drunk but not drunk enough.

A girl's next to me drinking a beer. Her two friends are talking and she's listening, nodding her head when she's supposed to. I lean close to her and tell her she's an observer. She asks what I mean and I tell her I recognize what she is, that she takes it all in, watches everything, hears everything. I tell her she's probably the quietest of her friends. She smiles and tells me I'm probably right. I pay for my drink, touch my plastic cup against her plastic cup. It's an upscale place.

"Cheers."

"To better days," she says and she doesn't look like she's just talking.

"It's another world these days."

"It is," she says. "But you have to live life."

"That's a cliché. I know you know that."

"I'm an observer and I speak in clichés. You've figured me out."

"And you're a quick study."

"There's truth to every cliché. You can be skeptical, but I think there's truth to this one."

"I'm not living life these days."

"You're alive, aren't you?"

Many days, many moments of many days, I feel dead. I feel everyone's dead, that everyone died that day. Or I feel the ones who died aren't dead. It's a dream. Or the wish of a dream that we're all dead or not dead, that we're all in the same place.

"Aren't you?" she says.

"I'm here."

"I see that."

"I wasn't down there."

"I wasn't there either," she says.

"Can you imagine being on one of the top floors?

Thinking that maybe you have a chance. That the flames will have to die down sooner or later and the helicopters will come and save you. And you're holding on, trying to take the heat, trying not to breathe the smoke, trying to ignore the people jumping out the windows, thinking it's possible to make it out, that you're still alive, that it can't get any worse, and then you feel the building start to shake and you start dropping. Everything starts dropping. Can you imagine what that must have felt like?"

"I can't," she says.

"Or can you imagine being on that plane? You know your plane's been hijacked, and there's going to be some ransom demands, there's going to be some trouble, one of those hostage situations you've heard about, and you're looking out the window and thinking how you're probably going to land soon, you're flying so low you have to land soon, and then you're right over Manhattan, you're practically in Manhattan, and those towers are getting closer and closer and closer and you realize you're not landing, you're not being held hostage, you're going straight into the towers. You're on a plane and you're going hundreds of miles an hour into one of the tallest buildings in the world and there comes that point when you realize there's nothing you can do and the tower's getting closer. Can you imagine that?"

"No. I can't."

"Or can you imagine sitting at your desk? That's the one I imagine most of all. You're sitting at your desk, you're trying to do your work, just another morning at the office, and you hear the noise of engines and you look up and there's a plane coming at you. Like in a movie. Like you're sitting at the movies and there's a scene where a plane's coming at you only it isn't a scene. There's not even enough time to move. It just comes at you and all you can do is sit there and wait out those few seconds before it hits. Can you imagine that?"

"I don't want to imagine it."

"I do. I think everyone should imagine it every day. I think everyone should remember what those fuckers did every day."

The girl is taking me in. I'm drunk. I never look as drunk as I am. But she can see I'm drunk.

"You're an observer," I say. "You're watching me closely."

"I'm listening to you."

"Are you a Yankees fan?"

"They're not doing too well," she says.

"They're going to lose."

"We'll see."

"Give me a kiss," I say.

"Why?"

She stays looking at me so I kiss her cheek. She's sweet enough to say thank-you. I ask the girl for her number and she takes a card from her bag and gives it to me. I don't bother looking at the name or the company. I tell her to keep observing the world.

I go back to Garrett and his friend. They're talking about a malpractice case they're working on, some greedy doctor who operated on an overweight woman who shouldn't have had the operation. The woman's now missing half her intestines and she's been shitting uncontrollably ever since. It's the stuff of easy jokes. Wheel her into the courtroom in a shit-filled wheelbarrow to win the case. Wear a gas mask during the trial to sway the jury. I've only heard a few jokes about the World Trade Center. Even the most irreverent people are keeping quiet.

"I hope they settle," Garrett says. "I hope they give us a million bucks."

"They're not going to settle for a million dollars," Garrett's friend says.

"Then we'll go to trial and kick some ass and the jury will award us ten million."

"That's a realistic possibility," his friend says.

Garrett turns to me. "Did you get her number? She's cute."

"I need to get drunk."

"You are drunk."

"Cheers," I say.

"I have to get a woman," Garrett says. "I don't know what's wrong with me. Do you know how long it's been since I got laid? I've got to get my confidence back."

"Why don't you buy me a drink and I'll tell you the secret to getting a beautiful woman."

"I thought you said there is no secret."

"That's the secret. Now get me a drink."

Garrett goes to the bar to buy another round. Mel's at a

dinner party at Le Cirque. Not with Junkins, with another man, a man she met when she was out with Junkins. Plastic cups or finest crystal, it's still alcohol, still helps, warm at first, at least. I look at all the women drinking and try to subtract the number in love, truly in love, all-or-nothing love. When he met her, he touched her eyelids. Now she's at a party. Garrett returns with the drinks and I down mine.

"That's the secret," I say.

"I need some secrets," Garrett says. "I need something."

The bar's drunken loud. Knoblauch strikes out on a high fastball. Randy Johnson throws strike after strike, effortlessly, his long body an exaggerated whip.

Applause. It can't be for the game. I turn around and twenty firefighters are walking through the bar in their dress uniforms, showered and shaved, not on-the-job dirty. They're the new heroes. Some of the firemen raise their hands in humility, clenching their mouths in dour straight lines. It's what they think they're supposed to do. And as soon as the first pretty woman talks them up, they'll forget grieving-etiquette and their cocks will go hard.

"There's a secret," I say.

"I have to get one of those uniforms," Garrett says.

"Who needs another?"

"Slow down," Garrett says. "The night just started."

"I don't want to slow down."

I'm at the bar trying to make eye contact with the bartender and he's figuring out some credit card bullshit, working slow motion, and I need my drink and he sees me, hands the receipt to a guy, sees me, pours a beer for a guy, comes over, lines up three plastic cups, pours three bourbon shots on the house. I put down a tip. The girl, the observing girl, is observing a fireman talking to her friends. He's got good arms, a buzz cut of brown hair, all-American handsome, bright eyes, healthy eyes.

I walk the shots over to Garrett and his friend.

"They're on the house," I say.

We down them. Sweet heat against my throat.

Time skips.

Finally.

Space skips. Just a few feet, but I'm there, in front of the fireman.

"It's a bird. It's a plane."

"What?" the fireman says.

"It's Superman. In the flesh."

He's been hearing so much adulation he can't quite believe I'm mocking him.

"The whole firehouse come out tonight?" I say.

"A lot of the guys are here."

The fireman goes back to the girls, but I'm not done. Paul called me a little man.

"Tell me something, Superman."

"Tell you what?" the fireman says.

"I see a lot of the guys here. But were a lot of the guys there?"

The fireman looks at me with his clear baby-blues. He wants to hit me. I see the flutter in his biceps but not in his shoulder so it's so far, so good. I have that nervous feeling like before a fight. I don't move. Paul's words don't let me move. He was talking about more than a barroom brawl, but not completely, and I'm standing here.

"If we'd been in New York City, we would have been there," the fireman says. "We're not from New York City, so we weren't. We're from LA. We're LAFD."

"What's the joke?"

"What?"

"What's the joke?"

"What are you talking about?

"What's the joke? "

The fireman's not sure what to do.

"When I say it three times it sounds crazy," I say. "Three's always a good set-up, even for a joke. LAFD. Laugh D. It says so right on your uniform. I wasn't paying attention. So what are you doing in New York?"

"We're here to support our brothers."

"Which brothers would those be?"

"The other firemen. Do you mind?"

"Really, do you mind?" one of the girls says.

"Do I mind they're supporting their brothers? Not at all."

I'm still looking at the fireman, my slit eyes on his clear blues.

"It's time for you to move on," he says.

"I live here."

"You don't live in this bar."

"Welcome to my home."

"I said move on."

"I'm curious. Is this part of your brotherly support? Going out. Getting drunk. Making moves on New York City women. Is this how you pay your respects? Is this how it's done in the City of Angels?"

"Are you looking to get hurt?" the fireman says.

Men in uniform. Thinking they're strong by wearing tight-fitting clothes. I once dressed up in uniform. We both dressed up. It was Fleet Week. The ships had come in and Paul and I rented a couple of sailor uniforms and wandered around Manhattan like we were lost, asking women for directions, then taking them to bars. This was before Mel. This was when we first met in acting class. We put on our uniforms and we became sailors. I felt mighty in my admiral's cap, my shoulders extra square in epaulettes, my biceps defined in perfectly-cut sleeves. So I know how mighty this fireman's feeling. He has his dress uniform on. He thinks he has a cause, why he's here in our city. And he has twenty brothers worth of back-up and a whole slew of dead brothers pumping his muscles full of bravery.

"You want some real trouble?" he says.

"After what happened, your trouble's nothing."

"I said move."

"When you dressed up in your uniform tonight, you and your brothers, you weren't thinking about the men who died. Admit it. You weren't thinking about the heat or the falling steel or the fear or the pain. You were thinking how women love a man in uniform. You were thinking you were sure to get laid."

"Move."

"Is that your answer?"

"I was there today."

"I'm here every day. The towers fell and you figured you'd come to New York and get fucked."

"Move," the fireman yells, loud enough to quiet the bar, loud enough to get three of his brothers to stand by his side. Suddenly the play-by-play is loud and clear on the TVs all around.

"Strike three," the announcer says.

I'm dead. A piece of life here. A piece of life there. Time skipping like my whole past was drunk. When the planes hit I ran downtown. I had to get close, had to get close to him. But I couldn't get close to him. I got close enough to count down the floors. I got close enough to see the steel melting. I prayed. I clenched my hands and prayed. And the first tower fell. And the second tower fell. And I stopped praying.

"Fuck you," I say and my words fill the space.

I want time to skip. To skip and skip but I'm here, still here.

I'm still looking at the fireman who wasn't here when it happened. His LAFD brothers are background. I'm looking at the fireman's shoulder to see the muscle twitch. I'm not that drunk yet. I am, but I'm not. It's an old fight trick. The shoulder twitches and the punch follows, but if you can read it, if you can see that muscle twitch, you can duck and come back with a punch of your own. It's the unexpected shot that takes a man down. It was the unexpected shot that took the towers down. Bin Laden knew his fight tricks. If Bin Laden were in front of me I wouldn't wait to counter punch. I'd beat him until my hands broke. Until his head caved in. Until my anger was exhausted, all of it, on the head of a hateful man. But he's not here.

"Move," the fireman says and grabs my shirt.

I grab his shirt.

We're holding on to each other. Standing there. Eyes to eyes.

"I'm here to meet women," I say. "I'm here to forget. Just like you. But I admit it. I admit I'm a little man these days. I'm not wearing some bullshit uniform pretending I was a fucking hero to increase my odds." His grip tightens. I tighten my grip. Hands holding each other. "Admit it. You're not a hero. I'm not a hero and you're not a hero. I admit it. I wasn't a hero. I couldn't do a fucking thing. And neither could they. And neither could you. Admit it."

"They were heroes."

"No. They were firemen. That was their job."

"He's right." It's not a man's voice. It's a woman's voice, a familiar-sounding woman's voice, an observant-sounding woman's voice. It's the observer and the last notes of a be-tween-inning commercial end.

"Look at you," she says, and she's not talking to me. She's talking to the fireman. She's observing the fireman. My eyes are watching her eyes and her eyes are steady.

"Look at all of you," she says. "I've been going to bars every night since September 11th and it's the same thing everywhere. You're all over the place. All of you in uniform, all of you drinking, all of you talking about the brothers you lost, but every day there's less talk about them and more talk about everyday life. That's fine. That's natural. But don't pretend you aren't enjoying your new status."

The firemen are looking at her. Their eyes look young, unsure, like kids who've been caught. The fireman I'm holding opens his mouth, but he doesn't say anything.

"They played the bagpipes for my father," she says. "You understand? He did his job and they played the bagpipes for him and if you asked him, if he was alive now and you asked him if he was a hero, he would have told you the truth. He was doing his job. That's all he was doing that day. He was doing the job he loved."

She looks at the firemen and then she walks around them and leaves the bar. The game comes back on. Men in uniforms. The play-by-play too loud. The fireman lets go of my shirt and I let go of his. I feel Garrett's hand on my shoulder.

"Let's go," he says.

I stay standing.

"Come on. Let's go."

"Paul called me a little man."

"You're tough," Garrett says. "Let's go."

I take Garrett's plastic cup, finish what's left, drop the

plastic cup on the floor, walk out to the street.

It's a clear night for New York City, another clear night in a string of clear nights. I can even see stars. There's no smoke in the air. Maybe we're too far uptown or maybe the wind is blowing downtown or maybe the downtown fires have cooled for the night. She's crouched down, my observer, like a catcher, leaning against the side of a building across the street. I run to her or think I run. Time skips. Space skips. All of a sudden I'm there.

"I'm sorry," I say. Her head is down and all I can see is her hair. "I was talking shit in there. I was drunk. I'm drunk. I'm sure you're very proud of what your father did."

She looks up at me and smiles.

"Do you have the card I gave you?" she says. "It wasn't real. I'll give you my real number."

I reach into my front pocket, take out my wallet, find her card, pull it out, give it to her.

She rips the card in two. Then she rips it in two again. And again. She rips the card into smaller and smaller pieces. She throws the pieces into the air. I see them and then I don't see them.

Like I had only imagined them.

Like the two towers.

They were there.

They were gone.

Like that.

Instead of running south, I run north toward the Intrepid. The World Trade Center used to be my destination, but now it's the old aircraft carrier, retired to museum status. The time makes the Intrepid seem more real, more war-ready, and I imagine the ship full of sailors ready to push off.

My pace is too slow, my legs too heavy, and only my heart is speeding from too much alcohol. I start to sweat it out. There's a runner in front of me and I catch him, pass him, run on. My heart slows. My legs lighten. I start to run, really run, and I stop focusing on my body and go to other things. It's like standing. I stand and go away. I run and go away. It's like drinking.

After I got home from the bar, after I dialed Paul's number and spoke to Paul's father, after he told me Paul was missing, I sat on my bed and didn't move. I didn't cry. I didn't scream. I didn't punch a wall. I sat there and didn't move.

Then the phone rang. It was my father calling from Massachusetts. We spoke twice a year. I called him for his birthday. He called me for mine. We had our own lives. He'd always had his own life and now I was all grown up, so two calls a year were enough. The attack warranted a third call. He thanked God I was okay. He told me to take care of myself. After he hung up I stayed sitting on my bed.

My best friend was missing. It was my first real loss, worse than when I lost my parents. I lost my parents the day my mother left home. I was in second grade and I don't remember much. I came home from school one day and she was gone. My father was stuck with me. One woman moved in with us and then another woman and after a while I felt like a weight, a dumbbell exercise to be done quickly so he could get on with his day. As soon as I finished high school I left. He didn't love me the way any kid needed to be loved and it was easy to leave.

My father took me to the bus station and that was the last time I saw him. When my mother left my father, she didn't say good-bye to me, so I don't know where her eyes would have gone. When my father dropped me at the bus station, anxious to be finally free, anxious to go back to the new woman in his life, he looked everywhere but at me.

I had spent too many years alone in my room, practicing in the mirror, dreaming of people looking at me, paying attention to me. Making-it was burned into me like a brand that couldn't be removed. I'd told Paul about my past, but he hadn't lived my past.

When the lights came on and the applause started it was a high. When I walked the runway, people watching me, it was a high. Even extra work was a high sometimes. Some movie would be shooting somewhere and I'd be on the side with the stars, and all those people who weren't trying to make it, who would never succeed or fail that way, looked at me. And standing at the Art Students League was a high. Hands poised, waiting to put me down on paper. I knew they were false highs. But the making-it stayed. It stayed until that day when I sat on my bed and felt the reality of loss. The brand came off, a strange healing, impossible for real skin, and a different brand burned into me. Loss. Forever loss. I was ready to change. I was ready to try. But it didn't matter. Paul was dead.

I stopped auditioning. I stopped walking runways.

The only thing I do is stand. I stand and listen to charcoal pressed against paper. It's hard to move these days so standing is perfect. I stand and my head goes away.

He called and left messages. I didn't call him back. He wrote me a letter. I threw the letter away. I was going to contact him. I was going to. It was in my head all the time, but with each passing day I felt meeting Paul, my best, my only friend, would be more and more awkward and I was afraid of that. Afraid of what I might say. Afraid of what I might do. Or not do. Afraid he would see me and not care anymore. I was afraid. But I was going to contact him soon. I had to, had to be man enough to accept the overtures that Paul was man enough to make. Days passed. Days and days and more days. I was going to contact him. I was going to. And I was going to be man enough in the best way. I was going to open my eyes and try to live. I was.

I sat on the bed with my father's voice in the room even after he hung up, my father thanking God I was okay. I didn't tell him about Paul. He didn't know Paul. He didn't know me.

I'm almost at the Intrepid. I can see the fighter planes on deck and the tourists walking around. I blur my eyes and pretend they're sailors and then I make my eyes clear again. I run until I'm parallel to the Intrepid, at the very center of the bow pointed into the pier, and I stop, turn, start running downtown.

I'm running. I'm thinking about fathers. How fathers should treat their kids. How fathers should look at their kids, eyes to eyes. Mel will never be a parent to Paul's child. But if she were, if all the factors that led to Paul's death hadn't happened, she would be a good mother. She can look at you and make you feel like you're the only one in the world. Even if it's not true, she can make you feel that way. And with her child, it would be true. She would look at her child for as long as her child needed.

I'm running, fast and fast, look-at-me fast, and soon I'll be standing, look-at-me standing, the sound of charcoal against paper, drawing my lines, and Paul's telling me to be me, me, and it's me running, trying to run past my past, trying to run that fast, that fast, so fast it's so far behind me I can live.

I run and run.

But it's in front of me. The gap in downtown's horizon.

She's invited me out to Le Cirque.

We're at a big table, a banquet table really, and I'm drinking the best bourbon I've ever had. The bourbon's so smooth, so rich against my tongue it could be cognac, but it still has the charcoal flavor of bourbon, the aftertaste of something carefully aged, and I wonder if the time skips will be smoother when time starts skipping, if I'll just skip right through everything.

The Arab looks naturally lean. Underneath his expensive suit, it's easy to see he's in shape for his age. His dark hair is cut close to his head, barely salted with gray. He has perfect, smooth skin. His jaw is strong. His face is all confidence and health. But it's his eyes that hold me. Sparkling brown eyes with flecks of blue inside set against the whitest whites. And they're intelligent eyes, sharp and calm at the same time, a calm that must come from the safety of money.

I count fifteen people. There's me. There's Mel. There's The Arab. There are Arabic men and American men, all in expensive-looking suits and silk ties. There are Arabic women dressed in clothes I've only seen on runways and American women, also beautifully dressed. The Arab says something and they listen. The Arab says something and they laugh. It's clear who's picking up the tab, but it's more than that. What he says is genuinely interesting. What he says is genuinely funny. He's the most charming man I've ever seen work a table. I try to pick out the moments of artifice, but he's like a true star. He doesn't seem to be working at all.

The waiters keep coming. The wine keeps coming, French bottles with vintage dates. The wine list itself, added up, would equal a year's worth of standing at an art school. The Arab's telling a story about his senior year at Princeton and a Music Appreciation final. I'm waiting for time to start skipping.

"Neither one of my roommates had studied, but they weren't too worried. It was a pass/fail class and all you had to do was listen to a piece of music, identify the composer and write a small paragraph about the composer's place in history. The professor told us exactly what he'd be asking on the final, so it was simply a matter of going over class notes and listening to the music. This was the last final of our college careers and we were looking forward to graduation. We'd been celebrating prematurely, but my roommates had been celebrating prematurely the entire semester. They'd skipped all of their classes and I know for a fact that they'd never listened to any of the assigned music. They both figured they'd pull an all-nighter before the final exam and squeak by with a low pass. The night before the final, they came to my room and asked me to teach them the entire course. They were still feeling pretty confident about the whole thing. I showed them my notes and tried to help them as much as I could, but they knew nothing about classical music. My roommate Chazz couldn't even pronounce Beethoven. And they were still drunk from a happy hour they'd come from, so they couldn't concentrate on anything I was saying. They both ended up passing out instead of pulling their planned all-nighter.

"The final exam was held in a large lecture hall with hundreds of students spread over the room. I put on my headphones, listened to the music selections and started writing in my blue book. About halfway through the exam, I decided to see how my roommates were doing. On one side of the hall, Chazz was clearly struggling. His head was in his hands and he looked pained. He would scribble something, then put down his pen and start shaking his head. He was failing the test and he knew it. Then I looked to the other side of the lecture hall and found my other roommate. His name was Brian Closky. Brian Closky was a legend on campus. He'd turned his entire Princeton career into a party. Brian was the most irresponsible person I'd ever met, but he was also the happiest and it wasn't a false happiness either. Nothing bothered him. Brian hadn't gone to one Music class the whole semester. In fact, he'd never bought a single textbook during his whole academic career and he certainly hadn't bought the Music textbook. Yet there was Brian sitting comfortably in the lecture hall, leaning back in his chair, his headphones on, his eyes closed, a serene smile on his face, listening to classical music and thoroughly enjoying it. I'd never seen a man look so content as Brian looked that day. To me, that was truly impressive. Instead of worrying about the test, instead of shaking his head and wracking his brains, he simply accepted his fate, sat back, and enjoyed the music while he failed his final final. Whenever someone says *Live for the moment*, I always think of Brian Closky smiling serenely with his headphones on."

The table is laughing. I'm smiling, I have to admit, and Mel, working her third glass of wine, is smiling too.

"Whatever happened to Brian Closky?" an American says.

The Arab holds the moment, then points his finger at the American. "He became a music aficionado. Brian Closky lives to listen to Beethoven."

The laughter sounds like a party.

"*Carpe diem*," The Arab says. "Brian Closky became the poster child for *Carpe Diem*. Actually, Brian became a senior VP for Patek Philippe. I buy a new titanium watch from him every year, and every year he sends me a Christmas card with a picture of his family. He has two boys and I wonder if he tells them the story about his Music Appreciation final, or if he keeps that story secret and simply tells his boys to attend their classes and study hard."

"What do you do with all those Patek Philippes?" one of the Arabs says.

"I'm afraid I keep most of them in my watch drawer. I'm guilty of neglecting them the way a child neglects an old toy as soon as he gets a new one. The only difference is that my toys are titanium. And when I'm in Riyadh, I wear the same watch every day."

The appetizers come. Beautiful presentations of choice ingredients. The men dig in. The women eye their food as if it's a prize for their being beautiful, for having spent the day getting cleaned up, made-up, coifed and groomed and dressed for lunch at Le Cirque. Mel picks at her king prawns . My Caesar salad is just okay. But my bourbon is great and when the waiter comes over I lift my empty glass.

He's back in no time with a fresh drink.

Appetizer plates are cleared. More wine is decanted. Mel is between The Arab and me. He's very attentive to her, asking if she enjoyed her shrimp, asking if she likes the wine. He touches her hand and she doesn't pull away.

The Arab leans closer to me. He's the main attraction here, the king at the head of the table, but when he leans in, he makes me feel like the three of us, just the three of us, are the only ones in the room while the rest of his guests are extras.

"Mel tells me you're an actor."

"I try."

I don't say *tried*. I don't use the past tense. I don't know this man.

"It must be very rewarding work," he says.

"Sometimes."

"I used to love the theater when I was a younger man. I even acted in a few college productions, but my family had other expectations for me."

"You seem to have done all right."

The Arab smiles. The blue flecks in his brown eyes soften and his face turns completely kind. He still looks the part of the king, but a king who would grant pardons to the guilty if they touched him somehow.

"I've done well," he says. "But as the saying goes, money can't buy everything."

"It bought you a drawer full of expensive watches."

"This is true. Yet it can't buy time. Even the best watch-

es can't undo that irony. And, of course, it can't buy love."
He's no longer talking to me, but to his credit he doesn't break eye contact.

"What's love when you can have titanium?" I say.

The Arab laughs. His teeth are straight and white, strong teeth.

"There have been times in my life when I might have agreed with you," he says.

"What changed?"

"Many things."

"What watch are you wearing today?" Mel says.

"My Tag." He pulls up his jacket to fully reveal the watch, thick silver against his fine wrist.

"Very sporty," Mel says.

"It's a diver's watch. It goes with my navy blue suit," he says as a joke.

Someone across the table belts out the punch-line to the story he's been telling and the laughter's loud on rich alcohol. Smooth, velvet-textured wines. Chilled, crisp champagne. The best bonded bourbon. I'm looking at one of the Arab women and she's looking at me. Her hair is perfect. Her make-up is perfect. Her outfit is perfect. A perfectly put-together Manhattan woman, but the model herself is Arab. Her smile, left over from the story, changes to something else.

The Arab woman turns her eyes to safer faces.

I lift my empty glass for a new drink.

"When I was a girl, I wanted a Cartier watch," Mel says.

"I saw a picture in a magazine of a beautiful skater wearing a Cartier. One of her legs was on the ice and one of her legs was in the air, and in the photograph it looked like she was the most content woman in the world and the whole world could have been ice. I practically begged my father for that watch."

"Did he buy it for you?" The Arab says.

"He gave me a watch, but not the one I wanted. It was a Cartier, but it wasn't that Cartier."

"Did you tell him?"

"I didn't."

"I would very much like to see that picture."

"I ripped it up when I got the wrong watch. I was a moody child."

The Arab smiles.

"The power of advertising," Mel says.

"The power of your advertising," he says. "I loved your portfolio."

"They're mostly meaningless images with meaningless slogans influencing people to buy things they don't need."

"Like Cartier watches," I say.

"Yes," Mel says.

The waiter delivers my drink, glass against tablecloth, a hush-sounding touch that softly punctuates the moment.

"I don't think it's meaningless to want something exactly the way you want it," The Arab says. "Or to know exactly what you want."

"Those are two very different things," Mel says. "You

can yearn for something and in the yearning it becomes a fantasy. Or you can have a fantasy and then when you find what you think is the reality of that fantasy, you can yearn for it."

"I'll need another bourbon to take that in," I say.

"I may need one as well," The Arab says and smiles and Mel smiles, lifts her wine, more goblet than glass here at Le Cirque, and drinks.

"What would you rather have?" Mel says. "Would you rather yearn for something so much that it becomes a fantasy, or would you rather see your fantasy turned reality and then yearn for that?"

"I would rather the second," he says.

"What if you could never have it?" Mel says.

"Then I would still know that sometimes a fantasy is not just a fantasy."

"Is it worth the hurt?"

"I don't know," he says.

"Have you ever been hurt?"

"I have. I believe I have."

Mel looks at him like he's the only man in the world and then she turns to me.

"What about you?" Mel says.

"What about me?"

"Which one? Which one would you rather have?"

"I'd rather yearn for something so much it becomes a fantasy and then yearn for the fantasy so much that I get it."

"That wasn't one of the choices," Mel says.

"I make my own choices," I say.

"But what if you can't have both?"

"All or nothing."

"David is an all-or-nothing man," Mel says.

"So I see," The Arab says.

"Do you?" I say.

"I can sense that about you. Like David against Goliath."

"Then you must know what my Goliath is."

"That I can't say. I'm afraid I don't know you well enough."

"Pretend."

"I don't pretend."

"What about you? Are you an all-or-nothing man?"

"I'm a businessman," he says. "Things aren't always that simple. Sometimes I have to negotiate."

"To get what you want."

"Exactly," he says.

"But you have to agree, sometimes the direct approach, the all-or-nothing approach, makes better headlines."

The Arab's eyes change for a moment, the blue particles seem to disappear into the brown, but only for a moment.

"I'm not out to make headlines," he says.

"What about you, Mel? Are you all or nothing? Were you all or nothing?"

"I'm the one asking the questions," she says and her eyes move around the table, to the other men, to the other women. They're watching her, aware each time she looks at them. Her eyes, so light these days, so light even in the mood lighting of Le Cirque, are less blue, more ice.

Mel's eyes return to her glass of wine. I eat my Arctic Char, cold things lining up in a row. An American across the table asks The Arab a question about the market and I lean close to her.

"Why are you here?"

"Not now."

"You can't be impressed by this."

"I'm not."

"I could be a real fuck right now. I could ask you all kinds of questions."

"Is that what you want to do?"

"Here's an easy one. Is it oil? Is it fields and fields of oil?"

"You're being hateful."

"Desert fields?"

"He doesn't talk about business. Not unless he's asked."

Mel looks around the restaurant. I look where she's looking. One table to the next table to the next. Then she looks at The Arab and then she looks at me.

"Le Cirque," she says.

I smell the red wine on her breath.

"The food's not that good."

"You're right," she says. "It's not that good."

"But I don't think you care."

"How's your bourbon?" she says.

"It's the best bourbon I've ever had."

The busboys clear dishes. The waiter asks if anyone wants more drinks. I lift my empty glass like I'm a regular at Le Cirque, another business lunch out.

Everyone orders dessert. They could be stuffed, sick, ready to puke rich puke or shit rich shit, but these gluttons aren't paying, and what's an expensive meal without an expensive dessert? I already know The Arab picks up every tab, every time. He's the king and that's what the king does.

Mel plays with her chocolate mousse. I drink my bourbon. The others drink cognac with their desserts, too sweet with too sweet.

The restaurant is clearing out. The different kings at the different tables need to return to their office thrones. The Arab mentions something about a meeting and asks one of the Americans if he has the numbers ready. The American says he does. The Arab puts his napkin on the table. Meal done.

The Arab gets up and the others follow his lead. Mel finishes her wine. She's the last to stand.

The maitre d' is holding The Arab's coat. The Arab smiles, confidential, kind, and I watch the maitre d' take in the smile and smile himself, as if he's been blessed. It's beyond subservience. "Thank you," he's saying. "We will see you soon, I hope."

"Of course. Everything was delicious. You must thank the chefs in the kitchen for me."

The maitre d' walks us to the door.

Cold sun hits the alcohol in my blood.

"Can I take you somewhere?"

The Arab's talking to me. Cars are lined up waiting.

"No thank you."

He shakes my hand. His grip is perfect and dry. "It was good to finally make your acquaintance."

"Thank you for lunch."

"My pleasure," he says. "I'm guessing you don't have to put up with lunches like these in your line of work. And it's true. The food is not that good. Still, Le Cirque has a name and, unfortunately, in today's world a name is worth quite a lot."

He smiles. Blue flecks in his eyes. He turns to one of the Americans.

Mel kisses me on the cheek.

"Thank you for coming," she says quietly, red-wine breath warm in my ear, like she's telling me a secret.

"Is this how you're going to do it?"

"Do what?"

"Is this how you're going to fall?"

Her eyes take me in and then don't.

"No," she says.

"I can catch you."

"Catch me," she says, flat, not a question, not a statement, just far away.

The Arab finishes his good-byes. Kisses. Handshakes. One of the Americans takes him around like they're the oldest, closest friends, fine suit pressing against fine suit. They could almost be brothers. The clothes he wears are western.

The food he eats. The woman he wants. Mel is standing there, perfect posture, the cold sun lighting her from behind. The Arab separates himself from the American. The Arab woman who looked at me across the table is watching me watching The Arab.

I turn away from her in time to see The Arab take Mel's elbow. He walks her to his Mercedes. A driver in uniform, standing at attention, holds the door.

My wallet's full with drinking cash and Trojan rubbers. I buy a pack of Big Red at the newsstand and, as is our ritual, I hold the quarter between my thumb and index finger until the owner is forced to snatch it from my American hand. I watch his eyes the whole time. Of course he doesn't say thank you.

I've already stopped in the liquor store for a small bottle of bourbon, now tucked in my pants, to get me to Float, the new midtown club. Free pass in my pocket. Promise of an open bar from seven to eight that clinched the deal. I slide my MetroCard, go through the turnstile, check the tunnel, swig some bourbon, a silent, mocking toast to tunnels that will soon be filled.

The subway comes. I stand. I drink.

I get off the subway, walk to the club, show the doorman my invite, go straight to the open bar to start time skipping. It's not Le Cirque bourbon. It's rack bourbon, open-bar shit, the name on the bottle not worth remembering.

The people come in. The bartenders work. The open bar ends. I pull out cash. I look along the bar. Hands on glasses. A watch on a wrist. Not titanium. Only 8:20. Alcohol slowing time before it skips and if time stayed right like this I'd be immortal.

I see the woman I want. She's standing between the bar and the dance floor drinking what looks like vodka on the rocks. No frou-frou shit for this woman, too much sweetness mixed in to cover the pure alcohol warmth. *Firewater*, I say, loud, a cartoon American Indian, and I don't care who hears.

I walk to her.

"Straight vodka?"

"Straight vodka over ice," she says.

"Russian vodka. Stoli. Not Absolut. That's my guess."

"Is it my accent?"

"It's your accent."

"Don't worry. I have my green card."

"I'm not worried. Ever get homesick?"

Her apathetic eyes soften, surprising since I'm just talking.

"There were problems in my country. I miss my family, not my homeland."

"Every country has its problems."

"This country has fewer problems than most."

"Not lately."

"Even lately," she says. "Things are easier here than you

know."

"I'm drunk," I say. "I'll leave it alone."

We drink. We dance. We kiss. I move my hand along her spine and she presses into me.

Time skips.

I'm in the bathroom.

A cell phone goes off, the ring counting time, no escape from the world. The man pissing next to me answers. After 9/11, phone companies cleaned up. If life could change in an instant, then loved ones had to be an instant away. I have no reason to get a cell. Before 9/11 if someone asked which person I'd call with a split-second call, a game like what-would-you-save-if-your-house-were-on-fire, I'd have known the answer immediately.

I breathe into the alcohol.

I was in Scene Study class. The teacher paired me with Paul the first day. The next day we met at the fountain in Washington Square and sat on the steps to rehearse our lines. I was dreaming look-at-me stardom. Paul had no dreams of Hollywood, no desire to make it. He thought it would be fun to do some acting. After our first rehearsal, I added Paul to the adage about never performing with animals and children. Animals and children and Paul were so uninhibited, so unconcerned about stakes, they played every moment naturally. All I cared about was that one moment of film that could immortalize me forever.

Our first scene was from *Days of Heaven*. Paul was the owner of the farm, a strong, stoical man. I was the traveler, hired on to work his fields. There were only a few lines to our movie scene. It was all about looks and pauses, what the acting teacher wanted us to study. When Paul said *That boy's like a son to me*, I felt it. He was really talking to me and so I was really listening to him. It was a moment, but not a moment about making it. It was a simple moment, two men talking simply. When we did the scene for class, I felt I should just keep listening, just keep standing there with Paul until he finished what he had to say. The teacher looked at us and then looked at the other students. He was an old man, frail and bone-thin, his voice a graveled rasp. During class he'd light one cigarette after another, sucking the smoke into his lungs before he spoke. He exhaled, tapped the ash and said *That, that, that, ladies and gentlemen, was acting because it wasn't acting at all.*

The guy pissing next to me is talking on his cell. "Are you there? I lost you. Are you there?" He closes the phone.

No escape. She's fucking him. Mel is fucking him. I see her drinking her drink, laughing her new laugh, too-open, right down her throat. A few months past, too few months, time fucking up, fast not fast, slow not slow.

"*That boy's like a son to me.*"

"What?"

He's still next to me. I've been talking out loud to myself.

"It's a line," I say.

"From what?"

"A movie. It wasn't my line." He's looking at me. "Did

you have a cell phone that day?"

"When?"

"That day. Did you forget that day already?"

"You mean when they attacked the World Trade Center?"

"That's what I mean."

"I had one."

"Who did you call?"

"I called my friend," he says.

"Your best friend."

"Yes."

"That's who I would have called."

"It's only natural."

"Are you drunk?" I say.

"I just got here."

"I drink," I say. "I drink and drink. It's the only way I know."

"Are you there?" I say.

"I'm here."

"See? No cell phone. And you're there."

I'm out of the bathroom and music takes over, bass beats and darkness and bodies in front of me, moving and moving, and I lean against a wall and press my fingers against my eyes. I watched them in the bar and looked away, knowing right there he'd disappear, and when I saw him again he told me about the woman whose eyelids he'd touched. He didn't tell me how he felt, but I heard how he felt when he described the simple things they'd done in the days I hadn't seen him. The neighborhoods they'd walked, the places they'd eaten and the places they'd drunk, the two days they'd taken off from work to stay in her apartment, which was open and light, and he told me how she'd grown up in a large house where everything was too tight, too polite and how her apartment was the opposite, open space, a few pieces of furniture, nothing that could break, white walls, floor-to-ceiling windows, sunlight all day. He told me the details like an actor studying for a part, making the details of her life real for him. I listened to him describe her past, her life in New York, the successful men she saw, happy to date one man for a while and then another, her choice to stay casual in a casual city, to work hard at her career, to live a focused and spare life, and then he stopped speaking of her past, the past he had made his own, and he never spoke about her past again, only the past with him, a new past, a past that started after he met me. He had always been happy in the now, but this was more, so new it needed its own starting point. I had never loved, but I loved Paul and I wanted this for him, this starting new, different from my starting new, which started with a bus trip to the city. He even looked new, his clear eyes more clear, his open face more open, and he wanted this for me, this new that made a week with this woman whose eyelids he'd touched, a week walking and eating and drinking and talking and sleeping, new and enough and complete and he talked and I listened and he wasn't saying lines.

I go back to the woman.

She lives in Brooklyn, near the ocean, where the Russians live. I ask how many Russians actually grew up near the ocean with all that land stretching farther than any American distance. She tells me she's Georgian, that Georgia is near the sea, that the Black Sea has resorts, that the Georgians fought the Russians and the Russians fought the Georgians, that terrorist attacks happened all the time, that 9/11 didn't shock her, that she used to be a scientist, that she lives alone with her daughter.

Her friend comes over, not as pretty, and says something I don't understand. It's a harsh-sounding language. The Georgian says something back, her voice not as hard.

"I think my friend is ready to leave."

"You're not having fun?" I say to the friend.

"I find this place rather boring."

"Rather better than staying home, don't you think?"

"I wouldn't necessarily say that."

"These days I'd rather necessarily be anywhere but in my room."

"That's you," she says.

"That is me."

The Georgian smiles. "What should we do?"

"I'd like to walk you home," I say.

Her friend rolls her eyes.

"My home is not walking distance," the Georgian says

I make a muscle for her. "I'm strong."

"I'm sure you're very strong. I drove my car here. We can drive instead."

"Into the sunset. Like a western movie."

"The sun has set. Come."

The three of us walk out of the club to where her car is parked. I'm not steady on my feet but pretend. She has a beat-up Ford Taurus with a bumper sticker that must have come with the car. *My Way is the Highway.* That's one philosophy. My way is the city street, Manhattan's city streets, a concentration of curbs and grates and hydrants and rush-hour parades that once seemed fun. Now the streets have memories of Paul but not Paul. Every time I remember something, the next thing I remember is Paul is dead. I want another drink, but we're out of the club. Driving. Streets. Paul. Not Paul. Mel. The Arab. I want time to skip. I need time to skip. A time skip like a horizontal fall. One place to another place. Skipping over memory.

She works through traffic, driving downtown and cross town, over the Brooklyn Bridge. I look at Manhattan's skyline. All those lights, like a chunk of heaven has fallen.

The scenery goes by. I don't know Brooklyn well.

We drive to the end of the borough. The car slows and stops and the friends say good night, kissing each other's cheeks. I get out of the car so I can sit in front. The friend is out of the car. She nods at me and I nod back. Her look says she dislikes most men. Her look says she dislikes men like me. I get in front. The Georgian smiles. I lean over and kiss her hard and then move away so she can start driving, so she can get me to her bedroom.

"You live far. You do this every day?"

"I don't drive to Manhattan usually. I take the subway to work."

"The office commute."

"If you want to call it that."

"Should I call it something else?"

"We can call it my office," she says.

"So what do you do in your so-called Manhattan office?"

"You really want to know?"

"Not really."

Her laugh is sweet. "Good," she says.

"Good. Now you have me interested."

"It's not that interesting."

"When I was a cosmonaut, I was bored out of my mind. Everyone was so fascinated, but they didn't know the half of it."

"A cosmonaut," she says. "I thought I recognized you from Soviet television."

"I miss the old country."

"But you're in the new country. The land of opportunity."

"And everyone hates us for that."

"Everyone hates everyone. The United States is not so special in that regard."

There's no traffic on these last streets in Brooklyn. She's a good driver, her hands comfortable on the wheel. She pushes through the yellow lights right before they rise red.

"What do you do that's so mysterious?"

"I work as a dominatrix," she says.

"Pleased to meet you."

I start laughing and she smiles.

"It's true," she says.

"I know it is. That's why it's funny."

"Are you going to make a joke now like everybody else?"

"Do you tell that many people?"

"I tell almost no one."

"You'll get no jokes here. It's a job. It doesn't interest me, but I'm sure you do well. Me, I'm a very dominant man."

"I can see."

"How do you say *thank-you* in Russian?"

"I'm not Russian. But it's *spasibo*."

"*Spasibo*," I say.

"You're welcome."

She looks at me and then back at the road.

"So what do you do?" she says.

"I stand for a living. I stand in front of art classes and people draw me. It's almost as interesting as being a cosmonaut except I don't move."

"A cosmonaut that does not speak Russian."

"That's where you come in."

"I wouldn't be a very good language teacher, but I'll give you one lesson. In Russian there are no articles. When I first studied English, I had the most problems with *the* and *a*. When you study Russian, you won't have to worry about this. I hated your American articles. I'm a scientist, I was a scientist, and I'm telling you there's no logic to your articles.

Language needs rules."

"No more rules," I say. "Not anymore. Not in the Big Apple. Not after what happened."

She pushes through a yellow light.

"Rules will come back," she says. "There was always fighting in Georgia and always threats of danger, but most days we forgot about these threats. My family is from Tbilisi where the situation was very bad, but usually our city felt like every other city."

I like the sound of her voice. I don't tell her this city isn't every city. I don't tell her to drive to the river, to imagine with me how the Statue of Liberty has to crane her copper neck, check flights coming in, aim her torch at planes flying too low. The Georgian's lived war. I don't tell her I imagine myself in a trench.

We pass a stretch of ugly, utilitarian buildings, Soviet-looking buildings, and she's looking at them, the soft look in her eyes.

She stops at a light. Turns. She stops at a stop sign. Turns.

"I suppose you rarely come to Brooklyn," she says.

"It feels like we're taking a trip."

"I hope you brought your passport. My husband knew someone in this neighborhood so we moved here."

"And now you're divorced?"

"Separated. Six months."

"Does he know what you do?"

"He doesn't care what I do. He's the father of my daughter and hardly that. We have nothing else together."

She cuts the wheel left and pulls into her driveway.

The house is small with a small yard. Before she turns off the headlights I see the grass needs mowing. We get out. The engine ticks down. The air is cleaner here than in Manhattan. I think I can smell the ocean.

The babysitter opens the door. She's about sixteen, her eyes so young and clear they look unused. I listen to her run down the babysitting checklist. Katya had grilled cheese for dinner. Katya watched some TV. They read two bedtime stories. Katya fell asleep at ten. The Georgian gives the babysitter a few bills collected from men who like to kiss heels, get their asses whipped, hang suspended from chains. The babysitter looks at me like I'm an intruder, then walks out the door. She must be a neighbor. The Georgian walks down the hall, opens Katya's door, peeks in, closes the door.

We sit on the living room couch and kiss. I undress her. Her breasts are large and firm and I'm sure they look great pressed together in a black leather corset, but with me they're unbounded, free. I slip my fingers inside her. She moves her hand through my hair. I put on a rubber. There's a rug on the floor and I move her off the couch and fuck her on the floor. She's pretty skilled. I turn her around. I fuck her from behind. I wait for time to skip, but it's not skipping. She's coming. I close my eyes. I see Mel. I fuck her harder. She comes. I come. I don't see through the world. Time doesn't skip.

I walk down the hall to the bathroom. I pull off the rubber, drop it in the toilet, piss, a game of hit-the-condom. I flush the toilet. The shower curtain's ripped. Around the tub half-used bottles of shampoo and conditioner, strands of hair circling the drain, a slow drip.

I open the bathroom door.

A kid is standing there.

Katya who ate her grilled cheese sandwich. Katya who watched TV and heard two bedtime stories and fell asleep at ten. Katya whose agenda wasn't supposed to include a man with his cock hanging out. Katya can't be more than six. She's wearing Cinderella pajamas and holding a stuffed animal, appropriately a dog. She looks at my cock, which is about eye-level for her. It's probably the first cock she's seen. The cock she'll compare all other cocks to for the rest of her life. It's a kid's perspective and no cock will ever look so big and so mean. She looks up at me.

"You stupid idiot," she says.

I don't say anything.

"You stupid idiot," she says, louder.

"Why don't you go back to bed?"

"I won't go back to bed."

I reach for a towel, but the damage has been done. She pulls back her arm and throws her stuffed animal at me. I catch the dog and hold it.

"You stupid idiot," she says.

Like mother, like daughter. I bet her Mom's submissive customers would get off on such sentiments. Katya picks up another stuffed animal from the floor and throws it at me. I block it with my hand. I remember the women when I was a kid, the women my father brought home. I never threw anything at them. I used to leave the house for as long as I could.

"Stupid idiot."

She keeps throwing stuffed animals at me. I'm the man with the cock. I'm the man that fucked her mother.

Her mother comes into the hallway. She yells at her daughter in English, yells that all the animals must be picked up or there will be no TV for a week. The daughter throws another animal at me.

"I hate you," Katya says to her mother. "I hate you. I hate you."

"That's enough. Let's get into bed."

"No."

Katya looks at me. She picks up an animal, throws it.

"I hate you, you stupid idiot."

"She's upset," her mother says.

"She's upset with the stupid idiot," I say.

There are stuffed animals all over the hallway, some on their sides, some on their backs, some behind me in the bathroom, but the first one is still in my hand, a small dog with a lolling red tongue.

She's just a mother in my eyes now. There's no reason to stay here anymore. Time didn't skip.

I walk to the living room and dress.

She comes into the living room. She looks tired in the

light.

"No rules," she says and smiles.

"Sorry about that."

"It's not your fault."

"I can't spend the night."

"You wouldn't have spent the night even if I didn't have a daughter."

"I've been having a hard time these days. I just need to go."

"Americans aren't used to hard days."

"After 9/11 we are."

"It's your first. There have been many 9/11s. Yours is not so special."

Katya starts banging something in her room. The Georgian looks at me, then goes to her daughter's bedroom.

I walk out of the house, mother and daughter screaming at each other my background music. I'm still holding onto the stuffed dog with the lolling red tongue. I'm not a collector of anything, but the dog's so perfect I keep it in my hand.

Body straight. Weight on back foot. Front foot slightly forward. The platform is cold to my feet.

Sounds of charcoal against paper.

The instructor is telling his students this position is called the classical contraposta. Like David. The famous

David.

I try to relax into the standing, but it's harder these days. The alcohol makes me shaky. Running every morning doesn't sweat my nights completely out. And what I picture, more still than moving, the picture of Mel with The Arab, doesn't get me away from myself, doesn't help me forget I'm standing still. The picture is color and not black and white, not charcoal on paper but flesh. And Paul comes into the picture. And the picture changes to my father, easy pop psychology. Loss connecting back to loss. Patterns so simple I almost laugh, but I don't laugh. I'm getting paid to stand silent. To stand still.

I was at the bus station, standing still, waiting for the bus to New York City. My father's eyes weren't still. He kept looking around like that would make the bus come sooner. He'd left the woman of the month at home. He was good enough to do that. The bus pulled in and he shook my hand and wished me luck. He was embarrassed around me, embarrassed that he'd chosen a woman over his son, that he'd given her and the hers before her all his time, all his attention. *Good luck.* Like he was talking to an acquaintance. I almost laughed at that too, but it wouldn't have come out like a laugh and my father's eyes kept looking around, looking everywhere except at me.

Charcoal against paper. Pages turning, one sketch finished, another sketch started. Lines and lines inspired by me, standing still, but not me. Just a body. Just bodies. The numbers on the news just numbers. Unless you lost someone. Then the numbers don't sound so cold, so body-less, so antiseptically statistical.

The instructor asks me to change position. I square my feet, twist my torso to the left, bend my head forward, put my hands on my hips, put my elbows out. I feel the blood go to my triceps, making my lines more defined.

Pages turn. Hands move.

"Look," the instructor says. "Really look."

There's no answer. The student, whatever student the instructor's talking to, is looking. I'm not looking. My head is down.

"Look closely at the trapezius muscle. It has its own arc."

Charcoal against paper.

"Much better," the instructor says. "See the difference?"

The instructor moves on. I stand still. Mel got into The Arab's Mercedes and I didn't wait to see the car drive off. My father wished me luck and I got onto the bus and my father waved once at the window where he thought I was sitting, but I wasn't sitting there and then he walked to his car and drove off before the bus left the station. When the bus pulled out I looked straight ahead, forward and forward until I was miles away.

The instructor asks me to change position.

I do.

A turbaned man leans against the subway doors. He has a knapsack over his shoulder and he's looking around the car with his dark eyes. The next stop is Times Square, the center of the city above ground where the ball drops every year for the world to see, and the center of the city below ground where subway lines converge in a colorful cluster on the subway map. The red 1, 2 and 3, the yellow N and R, the purple 7, the black-circled S, shuttle to points east. His turban is black. His skin is swarthy. His dark eyes dart. His knapsack looks heavy. It's only a matter of time before the suicide bombings start and the next stop is Times Square.

A white man's moving quickly through the car, eyes on the knapsack, moving people away. Fists clench. Shoulder dips. Punch. The man's head bounces off the subway door. His dark eyes go dull. His turban comes half off his head. His hair sticks out, so black it picks up the subway light, so long it unravels, and he slides down the door. The white man grabs the knapsack, opens it. Textbooks. It's full of textbooks.

He shouldn't have been wearing his turban.

He shouldn't have been looking around.

He shouldn't have been taking a train to Times Square during rush hour.

The turbaned man is lying on the subway floor, but nobody helps him.

"He's a Sikh," the woman next to me whispers. "He had as much to do with this as you or I."

She's old, her eyes more sad than afraid.

The train stops. Times Square. The doors open.

The white man steps over the man on the floor, just a body on a battlefield, and is gone.

We play phone tag, back and forth, the kind of tag where it's clear we're avoiding each other, where no one wants to be touched, tagged, you're it.

I pour another drink, maybe the fifth, maybe the sixth, my heart beating to rhythms amplified by Garrett's state-of-the-art speakers. He wants to tell me to slow down, but he doesn't. Instead he pours himself another vodka.

"Where are we going tonight?" Garrett says.

"Wherever they serve liquor."

"Every place serves liquor."

"Then let's go there."

"What about the Soho Grand? It should be crowded."

Garrett's face is flushed and his cheeks look too full, too well-fed. I see my face in close-up every time I walk into a bathroom, see the smudge of darkness under each eye like war paint, tired paint, drunk paint, and I don't even have to say his name. Garrett's back to life. He never seems to have left life. But he has his own sadness and I can't condemn him. He didn't really know Paul. I once saw Garrett standing alone on a Columbus Avenue corner, his hands behind his back, his eyes lonely, looking at the women walking past. I didn't approach him. It seemed like too private a moment. He would have been embarrassed, like I had walked through the fourth wall and broken his solitude.

"One more for the road," I say.

"Do you need one more?"

"I need to be drunk."

I walk over to his bar and help myself.

"They smell it on you," he says. "They smell the experience. Women know you know women, or at least the part of women you know. They smell that scent."

"There's only one smell these days."

"What's that?"

"The smell of mortality."

"That's why your philosophy works. That's the beauty of it. Hitting and running is the only behavior that makes sense these days. It's all about the right now and you never tell them anything else, so at least they know it's not a lie. You live for the moment."

"I don't."

"They smell it on you and they jump right in."

"Listen to me," I say.

But he's not listening. He's drunk and he's telling me he's got to get that scent.

"Listen to me," I say, loud this time.

"What?"

"Listen. It's a lie. It's a lie for me. I'm watching the now,

I'm watching myself in the now all the time, so how can I be in it? That's not living for the moment. Even when they bombed the buildings I was thinking how the steel looked like it was melting and how I'd say that one day. I wasn't just watching. I wasn't just there."

"You can't beat yourself up for that."

"I can beat myself up for everything."

"You need to stop."

"I can take it," I say and hit my stomach.

"Don't."

I hit myself again. "Right there. I can take it."

"You don't need to do some sort of penance," he says. "They're not your sins."

I hit myself again and maybe Paul should have hit me and maybe I should have hit him. It would have ended something, ended the talking, knocked the words right out, so the words wouldn't have lingered the way they had, bad lingering for me until I was embarrassed, too embarrassed to face him, look at him, like my fucking father hadn't looked at me. I should have hit him or he should have hit me and that would have been that. A fight. Then an embrace. Done. But we didn't hit each other. I hit myself, the easiest hit, no hits coming back, and Garrett tries to grab my arm, but he's no match for me. He's on the ground looking up and I hit myself and hit myself and start laughing, laughing and watching myself laughing, touched and not touched, and time skips.

"There," I say.

"There what?"

"I'm ready."

"What's so funny?"

"I'm ready. Let's go."

"You're crazy," Garrett says as if that would make it all right.

He gets off the floor. We go down. We go downtown.

The Soho Grand's packed. Film-biz, model-biz, artist-biz, business-biz hopefuls trying hard and enough A-list-looking women to make Garrett salivate. He approaches a blonde at the bar. She's fronting aloof but looking for a man who will buy her ten-dollar drinks, or, better yet, take her to eat at Le Cirque. Garrett asks how her night's going and she looks at him, his weak attempt, then looks past him.

I down my drink.

Skip.

I'm drinking another drink.

Skip.

My face is close to the blonde woman's face. "I wouldn't do that."

"Excuse me?" she says.

"Looking past him like that. It's not nice. And you won't find a more successful man in this place. He's just too nice to brag about his accomplishments two lines into the conversation."

"What makes him so successful?"

"Ask him."

"What makes you so successful?" she asks Garrett, suddenly interested, her eyes on his.

"Tell her about the bourbon list at Le Cirque," I say.

"It's wonderful," Garrett says like he means it and I admire his word choice, *wonderful*, the right combination of pretense and appreciation, a jaded aristocrat still young enough to feel. Garrett stands a little straighter and sucks in his gut. He's becoming the part.

I walk away, survey the crowd, buy another drink. Ten dollars gets me a two-count of bourbon, which I down as soon as the bartender pours. I hand him a twenty and he pours a five-count, happy to move on instead of waiting, bottle in hand, for my gulps to subside.

Time skips. I'm talking to a woman. Time skips. I'm talking to another woman. I see Garrett talking to his A-lister and she's laughing at something he's said and a woman behind me is saying it's so weird how a few blocks away all of it happened and it's true, it's a few blocks away and he's there, somewhere he's there, and she's uptown, somewhere, and time skips and I'm in the bathroom, pressing cold water into my eyes, blink, blink again and I punch the wall and time skips and I'm leaning over the A-list woman to get to Garrett.

"Give me your cell phone," I say.

"Your hand's bleeding."

"Give me your phone."

Garrett takes his phone from his pocket, hands it to me. I walk to the window, away from the bar, away from the crowd, a view of the street, people living their lives, and call

Mel. Four rings, then her message, not her. I call again. Her voice. Not her. I tell her I'm downtown, all the way downtown. I tell her I'm going there. I tell her she needs to join me, we need to smell the smoke, suck it into our lungs, she needs to call back, this number, now.

I stand by the window. Wait. Wait.

I'm in front of Garrett.

I'm giving him his phone.

I'm down the Soho Grand steps.

I'm down the street. My direction's clear. So clear it's lit up, the brightest place in the city. I'm running and the light's not just light but specific light, then one of the specific lights, and cops guard the fence and I'm the soldier, quiet and stealthy and quick and I see a piece of fence unguarded.

I climb up. I climb over.

I'm in.

Apocalypse. That's the word that comes. That's the word. Piles of debris, piles and piles, of things ripped and things burned and things crushed, steel beams and steel pieces, concrete chunks and concrete powder, all lit up by giant spotlights as if the biggest movie in the world were being filmed, but no actors, no director, no one yelling *Cut,* only men in hardhats digging, digging through the piles, digging through the wreck. A scene that's not a scene. Bulldozers with giant shovels. Trucks with full loads. Men looking for pieces of bone or flesh. I duck behind a pile, the color of something I've never seen. I watch. I breathe. I breathe in the stench of burnt metal, of incinerated flesh still smoldering underneath, all those floors compressed below me, all those bodies burned and crushed below me, and I gag and breathe in as hard as I can and puke. Wet puke, liquid alcohol puke. My puke mixes with the stench and I breathe in. The stench so bad it's concrete. I take it, swallow it, the stench working like a finger down my throat to puke everything out, but I don't use my finger, don't let myself. I suck the stench down my throat. I gag and gag and puke, bourbon and melted ice, whatever else lines my empty stomach, liquid splatting debris. My throat burns. My sweat goes cold. Goes cold again. Passes.

I lift my head. I look around. The digging is methodical. The workers do their appointed tasks. German Shepherds move over the piles. A lone, sharp barking, then quiet. The sweep of destruction so broad most cities could fit their skylines into this space.

The lights make it a false day. I sleep some nights. I don't sleep some nights. She goes out with The Arab some nights. She's out with him tonight. Or maybe another man. Or maybe she's just drinking, maybe just like me. I sleep some days. I don't sleep some days.

The lights. I look into the lights. The spotlight on me like I wanted. He said I was more. I spit the taste of puke and blur my eyes to the lights and the lights are flares streaking the sky and it smells like war. He's here. He's here and I need to carry him out. He's here and I need to save him. I need to save him for her. It's almost real. The dead are here. The lights are hot against my eyes like explosions and I breathe into my fear and reach for him and it's real. I reach for him.

Nothing.

Zero. Ground Zero.

Nothing else.

I sit.

The city, the city that's still standing, everything uptown and everything is uptown from here, is far away and dark, dark out there from the spotlights here. The way New York City lights hide stars and make the city the center, Ground Zero's lights hide the city and make the hole the center. All the light is here and I'm in the light. The line comes to me, the line I said when I studied hard, when I auditioned, when I cared about making it or at least pretended to care. *I am too much in the sun.* I am too much in the friend. She is too much in the husband. Or she should be. She should be here with me.

When I'm drunk it's like I'm in bursts of light, here and here and here and now I'm in the light and the alcohol is out of me, piled in its own small pile, and I lie down on this debris, lie down on this grave, lie and watch, hidden behind a steel beam, maybe part of the steel I watched that morning and thought it was melting, and I watch them dig in the light.

In the morning, in the real light, a police officer wakes me. I open my eyes. I'm in the fetal position, as innocent as the dead. I straighten my legs and stand. He doesn't question me. So I don't answer him.

I turn, a practical about-face. I walk to the edge of the apocalypse and out the fence. I walk uptown, my back to the rubble, the rubble on my back.

It's a rich man's caravan and she's on it. She calls me from this restaurant and that restaurant, every one a name I recognize, and last week her picture was in *New York*'s party section, The Arab with his arm around her waist, the blue in his eyes not picked up by the camera, the too-light of her eyes picked up too much. His name is Gibril Osman. He's listed as an executive from Saudi Arabia. Mel's listed as a friend. Sometimes she calls from her new cell phone, the drinks in her voice, and asks me to join them. Sometimes I don't and sometimes I do. I take a heavy breath before I walk through whatever restaurant door and into whatever dining room designed to make you forget you're in the city, rooms that separate the out-there from the in-here. Plush chairs. Spotless tablecloths. Crystal that pulls light. Substantial silverware. Ingredients arranged like art. The best bourbons in the world.

It's lunch. It's Le Cirque. Again. I raise my empty glass and like magic new bourbon appears.

The table's big. Americans. Arabs. Junkins is here this time, sitting across the table, nowhere near Mel. I'm next to Mel and she's telling a story about a man she dated when she first came to New York, a violinist in the Philharmonic who was arrested for stealing a Stradivarius. I've never heard the story before and I'm guessing it's just a story, but I'm not sure. I'm looking at Mel through alcohol eyes and the way first drinks make everything clear, I know I don't know her at all. She's Paul's wife. She was Paul's wife. That's all I know.

She has everyone's attention, as if she's paid attention to The Arab's technique, and she's telling how this violinist, this man she dated before Paul, stole a Stradivarius.

"He was a serious musician," Mel says. "He felt he deserved to play the best instrument in the world, but more than that, he felt the best instrument in the world deserved to be played. He believed the real crime was how this Stradivarius was sitting in some collector's house, untouched in a glass case. He stole the violin for the violin. He stole it so it could be played, and when they took him away in handcuffs he couldn't understand why he was being arrested for setting a Stradivarius free."

"What happened to this man?" The Arab says. I can see he's happy. I can see he's drawing her out, showing the table his prize can also talk, tell a story, entertain. She's usually quiet at these feasts, but today she's been animated since the appetizers arrived. Her eyes are lighter than ever.

"He took a plea," she says. "He returned the violin and left the city."

"How long did you see him?" Junkins says from across the table.

Junkins looks tired, like he's worked too hard, but it's more than work. He's been looking at Mel since he sat down, looking and looking and then he'll look at The Arab and back at Mel.

"I don't remember how long I saw him," she says.

"You don't remember?"

"I don't."

"Just another man?"

"I'd say he was less than just another man. I've never been a big fan of chamber music."

The table laughs. Junkins' mouth stays set, hard.

"He kept one of the strings," Mel says. "That I do remember. He returned the violin intact except for one of the strings."

Entrees are served. Wine is decanted. Whenever someone leaves the table for the bathroom, a waiter moves in, refolds the napkin, straightens the silverware, arranges the chair. When a drink glass is empty, like mine, it reappears full. Voila!

I turn to Mel.

"Did he really keep the string?" I say. "I don't know if it's a real story, but did he keep the string?"

"You don't care if it's real or not, do you?"

"Did he keep it?"

"Yes. He kept it."

The hard lines of the city are out there. We're in here.

So it's all a lie anyway. I blurred my eyes in the lights lighting up the digging and the memory is almost real like he was there and I was reaching for him.

A waiter walks by with a basket of bread. Another waiter walks by with a bottle of wine. Everyone at the table is talking and laughing.

"Le Cirque. They got it right. This place really is a fucking circus."

"Drink," she says.

"We shouldn't be here."

"Where should we be?"

"I feel dead."

Mel closes her eyes, then opens them, a moment more than a blink.

"Look at me," Mel says.

"That's the line I use."

"Look at me."

Her eyes don't move.

"You see how dead I am?" she says. "You see? But I'm not. I'm only dead now. And when some of the dead wears off, I'll remember more and more of him. Finish your drink. Order another one. I'm not judging you. I'm not judging myself. I can't right now. Finish your drink and pretend you're part of the party and pretend you're alive and after a while the pretending will drop away and you'll be alive."

"Do you believe that?"

"Make me believe it," she says.

I take her hand under the table. I press my thumb into

her palm. I watch her mouth. I watch her eyes. She isn't showing anything. I press harder. I feel the bone of her hand against my thumb and press. She squeezes her eyes shut. I let go of her hand.

"It doesn't prove anything," I say.

Mel breathes out the pain, an extra beat of exhale. Her eyes open. She turns to The Arab.

I finish my drink. It's a line I have to draw more substantial than charcoal. Drink enough to stay here. Don't drink so much time skips too fast. If time skips too fast I could miss her. Falling and falling. Different fallings. A body dropping from the sky. A high fly ball on the sunniest day, the ball almost lost in the blue, no clouds to create perspective, and you keep your hands steady and steady and you track the fall, watch the fall all the way, all the way until it falls into your glove. If you move your eyes for a moment it's lost.

I drink. I look at the faces. I look at the moving mouths. Talking business, talking current events, everyone skirting *the* news item, still the big news item. I'm watching Junkins. He's waiting. His jaw's tight, his eyes not happy. He's separated from Mel by a large white-tableclothed table, seated across when The Arab is seated next. Junkins puts down his drink, his jaw muscles relax and he leans forward. His tie touches the tablecloth.

"They found two more bodies today," Junkins says.

The Arab holds his own. He doesn't flinch. His eyes don't go harder or softer. His mouth remains calm. If I could see his hands, and one hand is on Mel's knee, I can see by the angle of his arm, I don't think his fingers would be clenched.

"Two more bodies," Junkins says. "After all this time. What does that make the official count? Does anyone know?"

No one says anything.

"They don't publicize the numbers as much as they should," Junkins says. "If I were a news anchor, I'd keep a running record of the count. I'd tally the count every day and end the newscast with the number of missing."

"The number of missing," Mel says.

Her voice stops Junkins.

"They'll never know the real number, Junk. You can't put a number on missing. You can't quantify that."

"You can put a number on how many people were lost."

"That's why you're a numbers man," Mel says.

"And a damn good one," Junkins says. "I'm saying they should broadcast the count."

"The count is too many. How's that?"

"Not good enough." Junkins leans forward some more. "What do the rest of you think? I mean really. What do the rest of you think? I'd like to know."

Junkins is looking at The Arab. Everyone's looking at The Arab. The Arabs are looking to see if The Arab will defend the cause and the Americans are looking to see if The Arab will apologize. The Arab's a businessman. Sometimes he has to negotiate. Mel lifts her wineglass and drinks. The

Arab looks straight at Junkins.

"I think that when all of this is over, when they have found the last body they can find, then you will get your count."

"My count?" Junkins says.

The Arab keeps his eyes on Junkins, steady.

"Tell me something," Junkins says. "How do you feel about this whole tragedy? How do you feel about this attack? We're all friends here. You can tell the truth."

"It's a tragedy," The Arab says.

"I heard another news item today," Junkins says. "There was an Arabic man beaten right on Fifth Avenue. He was standing in front of Tiffany's and someone attacked him and beat him so badly he's in critical condition. What do you think of that?"

"I think that's a tragedy as well," The Arab says.

"But it's natural. I mean, you did kill our innocent men and women. It's only natural we'd want some revenge."

"Revenge begets revenge. Hate breeds hate. You should read your history. Perhaps you should look at where this particular circle started."

"The circle is a hole in the ground. It's right downtown. That's the only place I need to look."

"Clearly."

"And they danced. All those people, all your people were dancing. You saw it. It was all over the news when it happened. It wasn't staged and it wasn't propaganda. They were dancing. That footage didn't lie just like the footage of the buildings going down didn't lie."

"Very few danced," The Arab says.

"I don't know about that. I saw a hell of a lot of people dancing. That's how much they hate us and that's how much I hate them now. If we blew up every fucking inch of Afghanistan, I think I'd start jumping up and down myself. It's war, after all. We're at war."

"It's not that simple," The Arab says.

"It's pretty simple to me," Junkins says. "We're at war. You killed us. We should kill you. By rights, we should kill all of you."

"Are you a killer?"

Junkins' face is red. He's leaning forward. But he doesn't answer.

"I didn't think so," The Arab says. "Your life is much too safe for that."

"What are you doing with her?" Junkins says.

"Finish your lunch."

"I'm asking you a question. What are you doing with her?"

"Control yourself."

"I am in control."

"I see."

"Would you like to see out-of-control?" Junkins says and stands. He loosens his tie. "If you want I can lose control and kick your Arab ass."

"Enough," Mel says.

Her voice is without expression, without anger or disgust or even urgency

"You should leave," she says.

"I'll leave when I decide to leave," Junkins says. "You should be ashamed of yourself."

"You're acting like a fool."

"You're acting like a whore. At least I have my self-respect."

"No," Mel says. "You don't. You're a broken-hearted little man. That's all this is about."

One of the Americans tries holding Junkins, but Junkins throws him off, circles the table, his hands fists. The Arab's standing in front of Mel. Junkins throws a surprisingly quick punch. The Arab stumbles. Junkins reaches for Mel and I'm out of my chair and he's gone. The Arab's driver has Junkins on the floor. The driver's hands are thick, one hand pressing Junkins' head against the floor, one hand twisting Junkins' arm behind his back. Junkins is kicking out his legs and the driver presses Junkins' head harder, presses his face into the floor. Junkins coughs, red-faced, red going purple, stops kicking. The Arab's still standing. He takes a neatly folded napkin from the table and wipes his bloodied lip. The maître d' asks The Arab if he should call the police. The Arab tells him everything is under control.

The driver lifts Junkins off the floor and walks him out of Le Cirque.

The Arab sits. The rest of the table sits.

Sorbet and flourless cake served on plates brushed with chocolate bring everyone back to civilization.

Mel excuses herself to the bathroom.

Dessert plates are cleared.

I go look for her.

She's standing at the bar. A glass of red wine half-finished. Her eyes far away. She holds a roll of lipstick and, distractedly, rolls it up and down, up and down.

"Do you know when I started wearing lipstick?" she says. "When I resumed my public life."

She puts on a coat of red, purses her lips, opens them. She rolls the lipstick up, *before*, rolls the lipstick down, *after*, like a spiral, like a twin helix of time. She closes the stick and puts it away.

"I slept there," I say.

Her eyes come into focus.

"What did you do?" she says.

"I slept at Ground Zero. That night you didn't call back. I went there and spent the night."

Mel's mouth opens just enough so I can see the line of darkness between her lips.

"Did you feel him?"

"I saw him."

"Did you touch him?"

I don't say anything.

"Well," she says.

She finishes her wine, puts the glass on the bar and walks back to the table. The Arab stands, like he's been waiting for her, the others stand, long live the king, and everyone starts to leave.

Cars are lined against the sidewalk. Most of them black. Most of them Mercedes. The driver stands by The Arab's car, his thick hands folded behind his back. There's no sign of Junkins.

I'm standing next to Mel on the sidewalk, her back to downtown.

"He wants to take a trip with me," she says.

"A trip?"

"He said I could bring a friend along. He thinks a friend would make me feel more comfortable. He thinks if I feel more comfortable, I'll be more comfortable with him."

"You're too comfortable with him."

"I'm as comfortable as I have to be."

"He's already in love with you."

"No. Not yet."

"What does that mean?"

"It means he's not yet in love with me."

"Do you care?"

"Care," she says like it's a word from another language, a word without meaning.

"What are you doing?"

"It makes the time go," she says. "I'm not going to apologize. I've never mourned before."

Her light blue eyes, too light, don't move.

"What would you suggest?" she says. "Do you want me to curl up in the fetal position and stay in bed all day? That's what I did. I regressed. I went all the way back. I was an infant for a few days, a helpless infant, and now I've regressed in another way. Now I'm back to what I was before. You never had a friend before. I never had a husband."

"You can't go back like that."

"I can. I can right now. Here we are. We're drinking and going through the motions and doing what we're doing. I might be excusing myself, but I don't think so, and I can't think about it now, and I'm not going to apologize. We're young and stupid even when we're not young and now I'm young again. The only difference is there's nothing romantic about this new kind of young. I'm young in a not-learning way, like what I had with Paul didn't happen yet. I've regressed that far."

I hear his laugh and their laughs. I don't bother looking, watching the handshakes, the hugs, the kisses, the post-restaurant ritual before they get in their cars. Mel's eyes, in the sun, are the palest blue.

"Your eyes look new."

"They're not," she says.

"They weren't that color before. They're the kind of blue that should have changed after a few days of life."

"See? I've regressed."

"If you know you've regressed, you haven't really regressed."

"I know I'm not apologizing."

"You're off the hook."

"No. I didn't say that. I said I'm not apologizing. That's what I said."

"I started drinking as soon as it happened. Not just

heavy drinking. Need drinking. As soon as his tower fell and I walked away, I started drinking. That's how I started mourning. More than I ever drank before."

"I like that," she says.

"Why would you like that?"

"It seems right."

I breathe into the alcohol.

"At least I'm alone."

"You've always been alone," she says. "But you're not alone at all. I know what you do."

"I wasn't married."

"No you weren't. So please don't talk about things you've never done."

I look at the line of darkness between her lips. Lip-sticked lips. For her public life.

"Where does he want to take you?"

"He has a place in the south of France. It's supposed to be quiet there now."

"The south of France. There's a cliché."

"Grief can be a cliché too."

"Did you used to travel with other men? Before?"

"It's not that simple."

"Then what is it?"

She doesn't say anything.

"Every meal is a fucking party," I say.

"I need to get out."

"That sounds simple enough."

Mel looks past me. The cars are lined up, waiting.

"It's not," she says.

"I can't help you if you're not here."

"If I'm not here, I won't need help. And if I'm wrong, I'll let you know."

Mel looks like she's going to say something else, but she doesn't. One of the waiting cars, black and sleek, pulls away from the curb into traffic.

"The south of France. I was there with Paul."

"I've seen the pictures," she says.

"One picture."

"One picture. One picture per place. At Cannes. The two of you doing your best James Dean for the camera."

"It's the only time I saw him do James Dean."

"He wasn't a rebel," she says. "Not that kind of rebel."

"An easy rebel like me."

"Stop."

"You know the photograph. You know how beautiful it is. And you know he was there."

"I haven't said I'd go."

"But you're thinking about going."

"Yes."

My hands are fists.

"I'm not going to Ground Zero," she says. "I'm not going down there. He was in the south of France. Maybe he'll come to me there."

"I blurred my eyes in the lights and I saw him and I tried to take him away."

"But you didn't touch him. And he didn't touch you."

Mel looks past me.

"Too soon," she says. "That's what you're thinking. If you were in New York when this happened, if you were in love in New York when this happened, it's not right to do anything but stay."

Another car pulls away from the curb.

"Ground Zero," she says. "It's not even a number."

Her eyes, so light maybe she wouldn't have to blur them, go from flat to something else, like she's going to turn, turn downtown, look downtown, and I ready myself to watch her, start watching her, watch her all the way into my hands, but she stays where she is, perfect posture, her back to the hole.

"So you spent the night there," she says.

Mel smiles and then her mouth relaxes and I can't tell if she's smiling or not. I can't tell. I can tell less and less about Mel.

Fifth Avenue is busy. On one side St. Patrick's Cathedral. On the other Atlas holds the world above his head. The sculpted world is a perfect sphere, an outline of rounded steel beams holding space. There are no countries.

The Arab called. Not his secretary. Not his personal assistant or one of his executive vice presidents. The Arab called and asked if I could meet them at three at the skating rink at Rockefeller Plaza. He said Mel wanted to go skating and it would be a change of pace from Le Cirque. I asked why he wanted me there and he said he had something to discuss.

I walk through the promenade that leads to the rink. The angels are still up, horns to their mouths, clarion calls to welcome their king, but the Christmas tree has been taken down, so it's a clear shot to Rockefeller Center's stone face, an Art Deco backdrop from another time. I look up at all those stories. Could the building take a plane's impact? Would Rockefeller Center fall? Maybe only the gold statue of Prometheus chained to the wall would last, the vultures feasting forever.

I see her immediately. She's skating alone, her posture perfect, gliding over the ice, her eyes far away. There's a man doing choreographed twirls in the middle of the rink and two girls dressed in short-skirted outfits skate backward with years of lessons already in their legs, but Mel takes all the focus. She's that beautiful and that far away. I see The Arab holding onto the rail, his feet splayed in rental skates, out of place in an expensive wool coat. But his face is calm and his eyes are sure. He's watching Mel.

I walk down the stairs and stand just behind The Arab. Mel skates around the far turn of the rink and then her eyes focus and she smiles and skates to me. The Arab turns around. Mel leans over the rail, kisses my cheek and I smell red wine.

"What are you doing here?"

"I asked David to join us," The Arab says. "Thank you

for coming."

His busted lip is almost healed. There's only a straight, thin line of red like someone took a razor and cut across his lower lip so quickly, so cleanly there wasn't any pain.

"Pick out a pair of ice skates," he says. "Tell the man at the counter you're with me."

"Go on," Mel says. "It will be fun. When I was a girl, I dreamed about skating at Rockefeller Center. I bet you never skated on the most famous rink in the world."

Mel skates off.

I go into the rental shop, get my skates, lace up. I haven't skated since I left Massachusetts. There was a makeshift rink in the woods, four boards surrounding a patch of ice, where I played hockey with kids from the neighborhood. We pretended we were the Boston Bruins, lifting our sticks in mock triumph or dramatically dropping our gloves to stage fights. I walk across the rubber mat and remember the tightness around my ankles, remember how to balance on blades. I step onto the ice and it comes back quickly. I don't look at The Arab when I skate past.

I catch up to Mel and she takes my arm.

"I mentioned skating once," she says. "I think he remembers everything I tell him. This morning he called and told me to meet him at Rockefeller Center."

"Very spontaneous."

"When did he call you?"

"Yesterday."

"Before me. I'm surprised he actually called. He didn't

say anything when I asked for you. To go with us, I mean."

"You asked for me?"

"He asked and I said your name. It just came out."

"Does he know I was Paul's friend before Paul met you? Did you tell him that?"

"Yes."

My fists are cold. I blow into them and the cold air smokes. "Why did he rent skates if he's not skating?"

"He skated for a while," she says. "He's actually not such a bad skater, but he said he preferred to watch."

"Do you prefer being watched?"

"When I was a girl I wanted to be watched, but all kids want that."

"I guess I never grew up."

"If all you wanted was to be looked at, you wouldn't be here."

We pass the two girls. They're doing Figure 8s. Their mouths are very serious, concentrating, concentrating.

"Look at them," Mel says.

"They're the real thing. They don't care if we're looking at them or not."

Mel and I skate, our strides pushed by the music playing over the speakers. It's a leftover song from Christmas. *I Saw Mommy Kissing Santa Claus.* When I was a kid, I never really knew what the song meant. The song changes to *Mona Lisa.* In the pauses between Nat King Cole's rich voice, the sound of skates cutting ice.

"My friend may try to win your companionship," she

says.

"Your friend?"

"I don't know what else to call him."

"I call him The Arab."

"He has a name, you know."

"Your friend can't win my companionship. He can't even buy it."

"The Arab," she says, slowly, like she's testing out the word.

"I'm guessing he's like the men you used to see."

"What makes you say that?"

"You've regressed. Remember? Or were you talking drunk?"

"I remember what I said."

"If you were talking drunk I would have wasted all that time thinking about regressing. You go back to what you know. You go back to what's safe. It's like curling up in the fetal position or sucking on your thumb."

"Are you done?"

"I'm still a kid. Forgive me if I can't control what I'm saying."

"I didn't say I was a kid. I said I was the worst kind of young."

"You're right. That's what you said. Back to before. You grew up with money, didn't you?"

"I grew up with some money."

"So that's what you knew."

"Are you done?"

Nat King Cole moves through the line. *Mona Lisa, Mona Lisa men have named you.*

"It was never the money," she says. "It was the steadiness that comes from knowing who you are. Those were the only men that ever interested me."

"Like Paul."

"Yes. Like Paul. And Paul was more."

"So you do remember that."

"Yes. I remember that. Are you done now?"

"Your friend. He's very good at getting what he wants, isn't he?"

Mel doesn't say anything.

"Steadiness."

"The strong kind. Not the mundane kind. Don't insult me."

"Thanks for clearing that up."

Nat King Cole's voice is warm and sad at the same time, the lyrics too fucking close.

"You would never take this trip, would you?" she says.

"Never."

"No matter what?"

I look at her and look at her and she moves her pale eyes away.

"I didn't think so," I say.

Mel keeps her eyes away.

We skate. Her posture is perfect.

We pass The Arab. We pass him again. I concentrate on keeping my skates perfectly straight. In Massachusetts I'd be dropping my gloves by now, squaring off, pretending a packed Boston Garden was chanting my name.

"You're right," she says. "He's very good at getting what he wants."

Mel skates off, faster than I guessed she could skate. Her speed doesn't take away her grace.

Mel slows and stops. I slow and stop. The Arab touches her cheek. The three of us stand together on skates. I could laugh. I could drop my gloves. I don't do anything.

"Well done," The Arab says. "You were flying"

"Only skating," Mel says.

"There was nothing only about it."

"When was the last time you skated?"

"I've never skated before in my life," he says, then smiles. "Perhaps two or three times."

"What about you, David?"

"Not since I was a kid."

"I skated once last year," she says.

The man at the center of the ice comes out of his spin and bows. Last year Mel was with Paul.

"I've passed this rink countless times," The Arab says. "Now that you've seen me skate, you understand why I always pass by."

"You did well," Mel says.

"As well as you lie. But you. You skate like an angel."

"No. Those two girls skate like angels."

"You skate beautifully."

"How did you manage to get David here?"

"I called him and he agreed to come."

"For an afternoon of skating," Mel says and looks at him.

"Okay," he says. "Not only for an afternoon of skating. I thought we'd get something to eat afterward and talk. I'm much more comfortable wearing shoes. I didn't grow up wearing skates."

"I haven't said yes or no," Mel says to me. "I haven't agreed to anything yet."

"So much for diplomatic small talk," The Arab says and smiles.

"Cut to the chase," I say.

"I rarely chase."

"Then why am I here?"

"Touché," he says.

"Fluent in French. You must have an easy time getting around France."

"We all could have an easy time getting around France. You'd be my guest."

"No thank you."

"I have a wonderful house in Villefranche overlooking the sea."

"I was in the south of France with Paul."

To his credit he doesn't blink. He has the perfect balance of calm and confidence.

"We traveled a lot together," I say.

"Mel told me."

"Did she?"

"Would you prefer I never talk about Paul to anybody but you?" Mel says.

"Maybe."

"I don't want to be that careful," she says. "If I have to be that careful, he'll become precious in the worst way. Like something you keep in a safety deposit box and look at just because it's valuable. I don't want that."

"No. You want to go to the south of France."

"I want both of you to go to the south of France," The Arab says.

"Why would you possibly want me there?" I say to The Arab.

"Mel enjoys your company. I enjoy Mel's company. I think it would be good for her to get away."

"To get away. That sounds easy."

"I'm not a fool," he says. "Of course it's not easy. We can never escape ourselves."

"Then maybe it's better to stick around. Maybe it's better not to pretend things can be easy."

"I'm not asking anyone to pretend anything."

"Right now the south of France doesn't even sound real."

"It's a trip," he says. "Sometimes getting away puts perspective on things. If you want to call that easy, then I don't believe easy is such a terrible thing."

A kid stops short, spraying ice against the boards.

"You play hockey?" I say to the kid.

The kid's young. He lifts an imaginary stick and shoots

an imaginary slap shot, then skates off.

"Think about it," The Arab says quietly, genuinely, as if it would be good for me too.

"I'm not leaving New York," I say.

"I understand. I did not mean to offend you."

"Maybe you need to put a perspective on things. Maybe you need to see things more clearly."

"I want to see Mel more clearly."

"Then look at her."

The Arab turns to look at Mel. He doesn't smile. She doesn't smile.

"I want to see her away from here," he says.

I study the blue flecks in his brown eyes. Blue and then brown. Not even the hint of a black outline, something to separate the colors.

"Have you ever been in love?" I say.

"Yes," he says. "I've been in love."

"Have you ever been in the kind of love where no matter what you do, you can't forget?"

"I don't know."

The attendants blow their whistles. It's time for everyone to clear the rink.

"And you?" Mel says.

"And me?" I say. "I'm getting off the ice."

"That's what Paul wanted for you most of all. He wanted you to fall in love."

"Paul's dead."

It stays there. The skaters are skating off.

"Well," she says.

The three of us are standing here, but it doesn't feel like the three of us. It's the two of us. It's the two of them. It's me and The Arab. It doesn't feel like three at all.

Mel's eyes come back. She looks straight at The Arab.

"Why?" Mel says.

"Why what?"

"Why? Don't tell me why it's good for me. Tell me why it's good for you. Why do you want me to leave New York?"

His pupils contract, and for a moment the blue flecks in his eyes thin. "I want to be with you."

"You're with me here."

"I want to be with you without downtown always being downtown."

Mel narrows her eyes like she's studying. Then she closes them. Her eyes were closed when I watched Paul touch her eyelids. Mel's eyes are closed and I keep my eyes open for Mel and I want to hit. I see her eyes moving behind her pupils, see the life there, and then they stop. She opens her eyes. She looks at him and she makes her eyes go warm. I've played eye games in the mirror my whole life, me looking at me.

She smiles at The Arab and when I look at him his eyes are back to before, the pupils calm, the blue flecks open. I'm sure he's not fooled, but he wants to be fooled. He wants Mel's eyes, her warm eyes, to be real and only on him.

"Let's get a drink," she says.

He smiles, but it's not a real smile. I see that too. It's a smoothing-over smile. "We can have a drink in the restaurant here. We can watch the skaters from the window."

"Perfect," she says.

Mel walks off the ice and into the rental area. The Arab follows her. I follow him. We sit on the benches to take off our skates and put on our shoes. I finish first and stand by the exit. Mel's watching me. I stay where I am.

We walk around to the restaurant. We're seated at a table by the window. The skaters we just skated with, seen through glass, waiting patiently for the Zamboni man to finish cleaning the ice, look out of focus.

The waiter takes our drink orders. The Arab asks if we want something to eat. I say No. Mel's watching the skaters. The Arab tells the waiter we'll just be drinking and the waiter walks away.

The window seat saves us from having to talk anymore. We sit there, the three of us, Mel next to the window, The Arab next to Mel, me across the table, all three of us looking out the window. The waiter brings the drinks. Two glasses of red wine. A bourbon on the rocks.

Mel lifts her glass.

"To our trip to France," she says.

"Are you being serious?" he says.

"Very serious," Mel says.

He touches her glass.

"What made you decide?" he says.

Mel looks out the window.

The Zamboni man makes his final turn. There's one

more path of ice to smooth and then he'll be done. The cut-up ice looks white against the new ice, the layer of water making the new ice look almost see-through.

My apartment is cold. I stand by the window. Even the concrete looks more brittle. There's no one out. I'm up too early.

I go down. The sky's clear, again, another perfect day for cleaning debris. As if God, having not intervened before, has at least made it easy, made some of it easy, after. Sunny days. Wind-less nights. No rain. No freezing temperatures or snow. The digging continues, ahead of schedule, and each time the news shows Ground Zero it looks more and more like a construction site. Too much of the horror is gone. No fire. No smoke. A homogenized mass grave. It must be the same way at Pearl Harbor. Or Hiroshima. What was war becomes peace, becomes peaceful. But in the coil of my testicles there's an angry residue and in places I can't even name, places inside my throat and behind my chest, I'm sad, and sometimes worse than sad, less than sad, a cavity of empty.

I walk to the West Side Highway where crowds gathered those first weeks to applaud the people driving to and from downtown, a strange parade of fire trucks, police cars, eighteen-wheelers, dump trucks, pick-ups, official insignias adorning vehicles from all over the country, coming to help.

The crowds have disappeared, but even now, where Christopher Street feeds into the highway, two people stand on the median, holding hand-painted thank-you signs, waving at the people driving to dig.

I walk uptown instead of down, my back to where it happened. Like Mel walks. Today she doesn't have to worry where she keeps her back. Today she's in Villefranche with The Arab.

I stop in front of the acting studio where Paul and I met, where we played our scene from *Days of Heaven*.

I stop in front of his apartment, where he lived before he met Mel, our starting point for so many city days and nights.

I stop at Columbus Circle, look up at the sky that's too clear, too blue, a tough day to pick up balls in the outfield, then down to where the lightning hit so close.

I stop in front of their apartment, where they moved when they were married, where Mel still lives.

I walk and remember other streets, other cities. For every trip we carried one disposable camera. Paul's rule to take one shot per place kept us looking at the scenery with real eyes and not through a lens. We traveled through Europe, a single Spartan bag on each of our backs. In Florence we ate so much gelato we both had to leave the hotel to walk off the scoops, practically crawling the quaint streets until we looked at each other, two sick gluttons, and started laughing. Paul handed our camera to a tourist walking by, grabbed two empty gelato cups from a garbage can and gave me one. Our snapshot: Standing in a Florentine piazza, gelato cups raised in a toast, looking like we're about to puke. In Pamplona we danced and drank and snuck into the stables to rile the bulls before they ran. Our snapshot: Staring at the camera, fingers above ears for horns, nostrils flaring, human bulls. In Berlin we sat atop a piece of the wall, legs straddling east and west, while we belted show tunes from *Cabaret.* Our snapshot: Straddling the Berlin Wall, mouths open in song. In Brussels, we pretended to piss on the famous Pissoir, mirroring the young boy peeing. Our snapshot: Pissing on the Pissoir. At the end of each day we'd find a café or a beer garden or a park bench and sit and talk and watch. I was mostly outside myself, just living.

On our last trip together, the trip right before he met Mel, we flew across country and rented a car to drive back. We traveled along the Oregon Coast, stopping at the most scenic cliffs with their pines and jutting rocks and wildflowers, hiking down to the beaches where sea lions sunned and sea urchins hid. Paul removed a sea urchin from a rock and chased me across the sand, the urchin's black spikes long and sharp. I picked up a rock and we faced off in mock battle. The people walking the beach walked around us, not sure if we were going to hurt each other. Without moving his eyes from mine, without moving his hand holding the sea urchin, Paul reached into his pocket with his other hand, pulled out our camera and asked an especially nervous couple to take our picture, just one.

We drove to Crater Lake, a space filled with water so

turquoise, so still, it looked unreal. We sat side by side looking down at the volcanic lake until our breath slowed, the slowest I'd ever breathed, that calm. We didn't use our camera there. The peace and the turquoise would never come out on film.

We drove to Death Valley. It was summer and signs warned tourists not to walk outside. Paul and I tested ourselves and ran into the valley where so many people had died. After a couple hundred yards the heat pressed our heads and backs, too heavy, and we turned back to the car. Paul stopped walking. His face had gone white and he started to sway. I held him, put him over my shoulder, got him to the car. I sat him down, started the car, blasted the air conditioner, forced water into his mouth. I took a shirt from my bag, soaked it, and rubbed the wet shirt over his forehead and across the back of his neck. His eyes came back. The color came back to his face. I told him he was fine. He told me to get my sweaty shirt off him and smiled.

One terrain became the next. We drove to LA. We drove to San Diego. We decided to check out Tijuana for the day. We parked our car in the tiny town of San Ysidro, on the American side of the border, as desolate and frontier-like as a border town should be. Illegal aliens lurked in the shadows, or at least they could have. There seemed to be no one around, only the far-away sounds of people full of tequila coming back to the States.

We walked across the border on a bridge made from depressingly-thick cement, past Indian-faced Mexican kids

begging for change, gum, anything, one young girl jug-
gling three bald tennis balls, another girl beating a worn
drum. Older women, mouths open, rotten-toothed, sat on
the cement sidelines and watched their kids do the work.
This was poverty. The homeless in New York could have
ruled here with their Hefty bags full of refundable cans. We
walked around Tijuana, saw a bullfight so close to the ring
we smelled the blood, ate a meal of pork tacos and guaca-
mole at an outdoor table, drank beer. Hustling salespeople
stood in front of the apothecaries and liquor stores, drugs
and booze the best buys in town.

It was dark when we got to the Tijuana arch. We walked
down a side street in the direction of the border and there
they were. Prostitutes stood in front of their respective mo-
tels ready for business. Some smiled, some pouted their
allure, some tried to catch our legs, snaring us with their
high-heels. Neither of us had ever seen so many women so
openly out there. I bought Paul another beer. I told him we
should get a couple of prostitutes, that it would be part of
our on-the-road experience, that it would be one of those
memories we wouldn't forget. I ordered shots of tequila
to make his decision easier. Maybe I wanted us to share a
carnal bond, to sample the oldest profession at the same
time. Maybe I wanted to show him what it was like to meet
a woman, sleep with her and leave. When he finished his
fourth tequila shot, Paul agreed.

We picked up two girls, and they were girls. They
couldn't have been more than sixteen. His a brunette with

pushed-up breasts and a broad face. Mine longer, almost gangly, her long hair brushed straight over her shoulder. When she walked along the sidewalk holding my hand, her steps were awkward in heels too high. A man walked past zipping his fly. We went into the motel, paid our five-dollar room fees to an old woman wearing a New York Giants cap. She handed us paper towels. Paul went into one room with his girl. I walked down the hall to another room with mine. A bed. A sheet. A pillow. A mirror on the wall.

I took off my clothes. She pulled up her dress. She was young, but her body was not young-beautiful. I looked past her pouch. Maybe she was pregnant. Her cunt looked clean. My cock looked clean. She leaned back. She opened her legs. I put on a rubber and started to fuck her. She looked off into the distance, past me, at some spot on the wall, perhaps at the same spot she always looked. She didn't speak a word of English except when she asked for the *dinero*, twenty dollars American before we started, another best buy in town. She stayed looking there, at that one spot, until I took her face in my hand and forced her to look me in the eyes while I fucked her.

"*Cerveza*," I said, because it was the only Spanish word I could remember and then a few more came to me.

"*Uno, dos, conquistador, cerveza.*"

She laughed at that. I was fucking her and we were laughing and then I held her head to keep her looking at me and I fucked her harder. She hardly knew how to fuck. I could have given her lessons, maybe helped her raise her fee. After a while she pulled her face away and looked at her watch, the international sign with a twist, time's up and time to come. I laughed at her, laughed to let her know I was as disconnected as she was. I started singing *Vaya Con Dios* and then I stopped singing, just fucked her, and shot my load to get my full twenty-dollars' worth.

I walked out of the motel. Paul was already standing on the sidewalk, the line of prostitutes behind him.

"Tijuana," I said like it was a fiesta. "How was it?"

"It was horrible."

A man and girl walked into the motel.

"Let's get out of here," he said.

We drove north. To Las Vegas. We stayed at the MGM, sat by the pool during the day, sat at the tables at night. Blackjack. Craps. Roulette.

We drove east. To Moab, Utah. Paul wanted to go white-water rafting. He'd researched the trip while at work, made a list of things he wanted to do, then ran the list by me. It all sounded great. We boarded a bus that took us to the canyon. A guide sat in front with a microphone and described the canyon's formation, pointing out geological features, then listing off movies they'd filmed on location. The canyon's cliffs became steeper. The rock was deep red, the color of an Edward Hopper painting I'd seen called *Early Sunday Morning*. The bus stopped and the rafts were waiting for us. I threw a stick into the water and watched it move downstream, bouncing across a patch of rocks, then disappearing. Paul wet his finger, put it in the air to mock-gauge the wind and shook his head in exaggerated fear. Most of the group was seated in a giant rubber raft, but the guide said we looked like strong swimmers and we'd enjoy the speed and bumps more in a two-man raft. We put on our life vests, grabbed our paddles and took off. At first we followed the big raft, but then we waited for the group to go ahead so the river felt like it was ours alone. We paddled hard into the white water and cried out in victory as the raft bounced and fell, the rocks rubbing against the raft, pushing against our feet, the water soaking us, spraying our eyes, making the speed feel faster. Between rapids, the water moved quickly, but calmly, the surface almost flat. We jumped into the river and let the water take us. Paul held the dock line so the raft wouldn't get away and the two of us floated forward, the canyon rising high on both sides, red rock then hot blue sky like in a Western movie, and we floated.

We drove east and north. To Arches National Park. To Santa Fe. To Boulder where we rented bikes and rode in the Rockies.

My favorite part of the trip was just driving. We were in between places, but it wasn't a skip. It was a connection. We'd talk. We'd sing with the radio. We'd watch the land go by. Even stopping at gas stations was fun. We'd get out of the car after driving for hours and stand still for a few seconds to enjoy the buzz of suddenly not speeding. The air, even mixed with gasoline, smelled different in every different place. We'd wash the windows fast, like we were a pit-stop crew. We'd get a candy bar or a soda. Then we'd switch drivers and get back on the highway. We didn't care about making time. Sometimes we drove slowly. Sometimes we drove fast. We watched for cops. When the road was completely straight and we could see for miles ahead, we'd test how fast the rental could move. Paul got the Pontiac up to 114. I got it to 115. Paul let me keep the record. As a prize, he bought me a mini-license plate at a truck stop with my name on it, DAVID in blue letters.

In Iowa we passed miles and miles of cornfields. Paul was driving and he pulled over and stopped in the breakdown lane. He opened his door and got out and surveyed the fields and I got out.

"Do you remember your lines?" he said.

"What lines?"

"From acting class. From *Days of Heaven*."

"I remember," I said and Paul started walking.

We walked deep into the fields until we were surrounded by stalks and leaves and the sweet smell of ripening corn. Paul became the farmer. I became the worker for hire. *That boy's like a son to me.* We finished the short scene. Paul ripped off an ear of corn, threw it to me, thanked me for my day's work and the line was real and we walked back to the car.

We drove to Chicago to see the Cubs play at Wrigley Field where the ivy-covered walls and sloped outfield looked so old-time it was like watching black-and-white clips come to colorful life. There was an air show in town for the weekend and when the first F-15 screamed over the stadium, I couldn't believe the sound or the speed. A couple of American Air Force fly-overs and any country with half a brain would concede defeat. It was impossible to concentrate on the game with all the power up there. F-15 after F-15 passed over the stadium and then a group of four in formation, and I imagined the bombs coming out, imagined the fear that comes when it's impossible to escape, when the speed is that fast, the noise that loud, the power that deadly. I pretended it was real war.

After the F-15s passed, Paul pointed to the sky and yelled a giddy *Damn*. A single stealth bomber flew toward us. It was wider than any plane I'd seen, one sleek triangle of a wing, and gigantic, filling the sky with a span of black right out of a *Batman* movie. The show ended and I imagined the end of war, right after, imagined the loss even in victory, and the sadness that must come in lower octaves, as deep as the saddest notes from a funeral bagpipe.

Before we pulled into New York City, thousands of miles behind us, our cross country drive almost done, we got stuck in traffic outside the Lincoln Tunnel. Paul was driving. I was in the passenger seat. It was stop-and-go, stop-and-go. Then traffic just stopped. Paul shifted into Park and turned to me and I saw there was something in his eyes more disappointed than coming to the end of a road trip. Paul asked me never to mention Tijuana to anyone. It was our secret, but it didn't feel like a good secret. I promised I never would.

After I fucked, after I came, I always felt I could see

through the world. My sperm depleted, my vision improved and I felt calmly powerful. I would lift myself off the woman and look straight ahead, seeing straight ahead, right through everything. When I saw Paul standing outside that Tijuana motel, I knew he wasn't seeing through the world. Paul had fucked a prostitute out of deference to me, out of friendship, to seal our on-the-road bond, which really didn't need sealing. And standing there, with a backdrop of girls for hire, the motel's neon sign reddening the sidewalk around his feet, I saw an expression I'd never seen on Paul. He was ashamed.

We'd driven three-thousand miles from Tijuana, but Tijuana was right there in his thoughts, right before we officially entered New York. He had felt the disconnection, the closed-eyed living that I lived, and it had stayed with him. The last time we spoke, the first time I ran away from him, the last time I saw him alive, he asked me to open my eyes.

I keep walking, a self-imposed forced march like a prisoner of war. If we are indeed at war, and that's what the president keeps saying, if we are really under constant threat, and that's what the news keeps saying, color-coded alerts every day, then I'm a prisoner and in the confines of my city, in the confines of my memories, I can walk here or walk there, but I'm not free to forget.

I walk forward to St. Vincent's Hospital.

On September 11th, that very day, the signs started going up, sheets of paper taped all over the city and every sheet the same, as if there were an official format for presenting World Trade Center victims.

Photograph.

Name.

Date of birth.

Physical description.

Employer.

Tower number.

Floor number.

And on top of each sheet was that one word printed in boldface.

MISSING.

The walls around every hospital were filled, paper overlapping paper, and that day, and days after, I would visit the different hospitals, look at the faces, read the small pieces of information, one by one by one. During those early days newscasters used the walls as perfect backdrops for brutally sad interviews. Family members broke down on camera. Newscasters broke down on camera. Cameramen broke down off camera. I heard the murmuring voices, grief and disbelief, as I walked from one end of each wall to the next. At every hospital the photographed faces were the same, literally. Some family members covered the city with faces of their missing, taped their desperate posters to phone booths, store windows, light poles, stop signs. MISSING. Of course, they weren't missing. Missing was just an optimistic euphemism. When the buildings fell I knew he was more than missing.

Paul's face was on every hospital's walls. Mel did what

she could even when there was nothing to be done. Those days just after, I looked for Paul's photograph and looked at Paul's photograph many times, the strong mouth, the kind eyes and then I moved down the wall, looked at other faces, strong and weak, at other eyes, kind and flirtatious and ambitious and lonely, and then I walked on.

When the towers went down, St. Vincent's was designated a triage center. Doctors and nurses in scrubs stood around the emergency room entrance waiting for the hurt to arrive. That's all they did. They waited. And they waited. And morning became afternoon. And no one arrived. If you were there, in the towers, that day, you weren't injured. You weren't missing. You were dead.

I walk along St. Vincent's wall. The photographs are still up, covered in protective plastic against the elements as if that could make them immortal. When I get near the place where his picture is posted, I stop walking and turn around.

I've seen the photograph too many times and don't like that his face in the photograph is taking over, that when I think of him the picture I see is that picture. I don't hope for many things these days, but I hope he'll come back, all of him, and that the photograph, that one photograph, colors too bright on copy paper, MISSING written above in Mel's bold letters, will become just a single picture, even if it is a final one, in a whole album of faces, Paul's different faces, in my head.

A cold sweat moves from my hands, up my arms, over my chest, across my back and there's nothing in me to hold me in place and the air there, the stench pressing into my throat, forced everything out and I don't remember days and I drank last night, I did drink last night, and the charcoal is moving, I hear that, and they're drawing body lines, I hear that, and I force myself not to fall and look at me.

The dream's still in me, pounded into my brain from alcohol evaporating there. It's the usual dream. I'm walking to a tall building and a plane's flying too low and it's clear what's going to happen. I turn and run. But I can't run fast enough. My legs are heavy and my stride is cartoon-useless, all effort but no movement forward. The plane hits. The building explodes. I see the ball of flame even while my back is turned, the long view of dreams.

I'm on my bed, breathing too fast, heart beating too fast, thirsty for water but sick from drinking water. There are so many skipped moments from last night it's not worth trying to connect the dots. I'm not even sure of the dots. I drank in my room and went out and drank and woke in my room, but in between I don't know. I just know the dream, but that's not real time. I just know she's with him in the south of France.

It's too hot in my room. I can't run, but maybe I can

walk. I go down and the street is quiet and my mouth's too dry and my breath's too fast, smoke in the cold. I'm near the newsstand. The Sunday papers are thick, stacked. I get my wallet from my pocket, get the money out, steady my hand. I don't want the newsstand Arab to see me shaking. I keep the money in my hand and make him reach. No *Thank you*. No *You're welcome*. I stand in front of his stand and open to the only pages I care about. On Sunday they write profiles of the 9/11 dead. A picture. A few words. A life summed up. Most of the faces are smile-for-the-camera happy. Paul hasn't appeared yet. Garret's classmate John appeared. *Johnny I hardly knew ya.*

I cross Seventh Avenue to get back to my apartment. And I see a woman I recognize. For a moment I flash to what I must look like from her perspective, this man who sits near The Arab on some of his caravan lunches, who sits carefully and listens carefully and even drinks carefully and walks after Mel when she walks away, most careful of all, now crossing the avenue still drunk in ripped jeans, a stained T-shirt, red-eyed and bourbon-beaten. The woman holds my eyes too long. She can't pretend she hasn't seen me, or that she doesn't know where she knows me from. Our eyes have met too often across the perfectly set table at Le Cirque. She's the Arab woman who watches me, her eyes almond-shaped and dark.

She was going to pass me on the avenue, just pass me, but etiquette stops her. Her mouth parts, she's thinking of what to say, and then she says it, slowly, so I can guess the words before she says them.

"You're Mel's friend."

"That's me." I breathe the bourbon down. "And you eat for free at Le Cirque."

I press my fingers into the newspaper to keep me here, to keep me from just lying down on the avenue, tucking my legs into my chest, sleeping off the hangover making me sick.

"We all eat for free at that table," she says.

"I drink more than I eat."

"I've noticed," she says.

"I'm flattered you pay such close attention. Do you notice anything now?"

"I can smell it on your breath."

"Very good. It's like I've already started. Do you want to join me for a drink?"

"You have a voice. You hardly ever talk at Le Cirque,"

"I don't need to talk there."

I'm breathing after every sentence, end-of-drunk exhausted.

"That table can't do anything for me," I say.

"Is that the only reason you talk to people?"

I'm hot and her voice is crisp like cold air, the cold I don't feel. The back of my hand is pale with cold.

"Sometimes I talk to create the dots," I say. "To figure out the time skips."

"The time skips?"

"Even at Le Cirque. There are parts I almost don't remember."

"One lunch blends into the next," she says.

I'm looking at my fingers, the ones not holding the paper, my nails dirty, my fingers bloated from booze. Running makes the swelling go down.

"That's the way business lunches are," she says.

"Those lunches aren't about business."

"Work gets done even at Le Cirque."

"Is that why you talk?"

"I'm human," she says. "I talk."

"What else do you do that's human?"

"I do things that interest me."

"Do you pray?"

"I'm not religious," she says.

"No more prayers."

I breathe. I look at my swollen fingers.

"I don't believe there are many religious people in finance," she says.

"What about your boss?"

"Gibril," she says. "And he's not my boss."

"Is he religious? Does he pray?"

"I don't know. He's devoted to his work. I'd say that's his religion."

"I'm still drunk." I say. "Does he love?"

I breathe. She breathes. But hers is slow.

"I don't know that either," she says.

"You don't know him very well, do you?"

"I know him well enough," she says.

"You know her husband died on 9/11?"

"Mel told me about her husband."

"He was my only friend."

"She mentioned you were close."

"Mel talks to you?"

"We talk sometimes."

"Does he talk to you?"

"Gibril?"

"He took her to France."

"I heard."

"What else did you hear?"

"That's all."

"Did he tell you or did Mel tell you?"

"He did," she says.

"Did he tell you he loved her?"

"He doesn't talk to me about love."

"Then he must love her. He's keeping her quiet. He's keeping her sacred."

The Arab woman's eyes are intelligent eyes. I wonder how many drinks it would take to turn them red-lined and dull.

"I warned Mel about him," she says.

"About what?"

"He likes many women."

"Does he like you?"

"I'm married."

"Does that stop him?"

"I knew Gibril before I was married. He respects my

marriage."

"But if your husband were freshly killed you'd be fair game?"

The woman doesn't say anything. I breathe, exhausted.

"Would you go off with him if your husband had just been killed?" I say. "Would you do that?"

Her eyes are clear.

"Would you?" I say.

A car horn goes off too loud, the cab too close, too fast. I grab her arm, pull her to the sidewalk and after she lifts her foot to the curb I know there's something to this moment, to this decision I've made without thinking that's different from what Mel did. She thought about it. She had time to think about it. And then she made the decision to go. I'm still drunk and I see it. I could hurt her for that. I could let her just fall, watch her all the way down, falling, falling, then hitting hard, concrete-cracking hard. I have too many daydreams when I'm still drunk, these-day dreams, dreaming violence.

She's standing on the sidewalk next to me. My hand's still around her arm.

"Thank you," she says.

"Savior of the day."

Her lips are full and soft-looking.

"She went to France," I say. "It's like a death bed promise. I promised I'd catch her. I promised I'd keep her safe. But it was a promise to my friend Paul. And he was dead already, so it wasn't really a death bed promise. And she's not dead. And I'm not dead. Not really. So it's not really a death bed promise, but it feels like one. It feels that heavy. It feels like that much weight."

"Perhaps she's relying on you even if she's not here."

"She went away to France with another man. And I'm still here."

I let go of her arm. I'm too cold and too hot.

"I'm still drunk," I say.

"You said."

"You were there the last time."

"Where?"

"The last time I was there. When that man Junkins went after your friend."

"He's a hateful man," she says.

"He is. He is a hateful man. But sometimes I hate too. Sometimes I can't help hating all of you for what happened."

She breathes in once.

"That's honest," she says.

"It's honest and it's hateful and sometimes I just want to hit just like him."

I'm breathing heavy. She is still, like her breath has stopped. I'm looking at her mouth to see if any smoke comes out. Then she breathes.

"Even so," she says. "You're not like that man."

She holds my eyes long enough to let me know it's a moment, smart enough to know that when you have a moment like this, the simplest look means everything. Simple. An American. An Arab. The hole a mile downtown. And they're miles away in the south of France.

Then she moves her dark eyes from mine and crosses the avenue.

I get a postcard from Mel. On the front a picture with *Cote D'Azur* in cursive. Mountains that go right to the Mediterranean. A crescent of sand-colored buildings. A beach with sunbathers. A sky so blue it looks fake. On the back, eight words.

PALM TREES. ROCK BEACHES. LONG WALKS. LONG NIGHTS.

Skipped spaces.
Standing.
Drinking.
Night to night to night.

The last shots of come are coming out and I hear my voice. *No.* It's not even all out and I'm back in these days. I get off the bed, put on my clothes and a woman, her face not fully the face I remember from the bar, more defined in dawn-light, is facing me. She looks like she wants to ask where I'm going. She pulls the sheet to her neck.

"I have to run."

"What does that mean?" she says.

"I just have to run."

"Nice," she says.

It's the damage Paul told me about. I may not promise anything, but they still feel and I stop.

"No," I say.

"No what?"

"It felt good. You felt good."

I go over and kiss her. I keep my mouth on her mouth, just long enough, and then move away and she doesn't say anything.

I put on my shoes, leave her apartment, take the elevator down.

It's cold and I see my breath. I'm sure it's warmer there, the Cote d'Azur, with its palm trees and rock beaches and the Mediterranean a different blue from any water I've ever seen. I don't know if she's walking alone. I don't know if her long nights are with The Arab. He has to be falling for her. She has to be drinking. I look at my hands and my fingers are swollen.

I look for a bodega for a Yoo-hoo to coat the hangover in my throat and stomach. I look at the sidewalk to keep my balance. My shoes are untied. I'm the guy walking deserted streets with untied shoes. Maybe this is how they start. The guys you see sitting on subway steps, hats covering their faces, fingers burnt from cigarette butts smoked too close, talking to themselves, memories so real they are real.

Like that.

I get a second postcard from Mel. The same postcard. Mountains and water and too-blue sky. The words *Cote d'Azur* in cursive.

On the back, seven words. One less than the last card.

TOO MUCH SUN. ONE PICTURE PER PLACE.

Things to worry about:

A Saudi flying a plane.

A Syrian driving a car.

A Muslim with explosives strapped to his chest.

An Arab with a vial of anthrax.

Too much sun in the south of France. Too much sun so she can see. Or too much sun that it gets in her eyes. Or too much sun that it works like a spotlight. Or too much sun that it burns.

I scan the subway car, but see no danger. I'm in my work clothes, the clothes I bring to the Art Students League, easy-off easy-on clothes. I stood and listened to the charcoal and couldn't get away, not even a little. I saw The Arab and I saw Mel and then I saw the Arab woman with her dark eyes. *You're not like that man*, she said, standing on Seventh

Avenue. *Little man*, Paul said, sitting in the bar. What would he call her now? *Little woman*? *Little wife*? Would he grab Mel and make her listen? Would she walk out? Would she walk out if she knew she'd never see him again? *That's what Paul wanted for you most of all. He wanted you to fall in love*, she said, standing on ice. He's dead and she left and I'm here and the subway stops and I run the stairs. I need to drink.

I go into a bar, drink one shot, drink another. There's no one here, nobody, nothing to help me create a border to my skipped spaces, to connect one moment to the next, blackout in between. The bartender's cutting limes for later. I push the door open with my work boot.

The city's too quiet, too early for rush hour, too late for late-lunch stragglers. Even Le Cirque must be done serving, the dining room empty, the tables already set for dinner, fresh linens and clean silverware, and the workers on break waiting for the kings to come.

I go into a bar. No one. I leave.

I walk to the newsstand, take a pack of Big Red, take a quarter from my pocket, hold the quarter until the Arab has to touch my hand.

The Arab tries to pry the quarter from my fingers.

"Tell me," I say.

"Tell you what?" he says. His voice is gentler than I imagined.

"How did you feel?"

He's trying to get the quarter.

"You took the gum," he says. "Give me the money."

"Tell me."

"Give me the money, asshole."

I'm pulling him, pulling him to me, pulling him out of his newsstand, his legs kicking, gum and candy spilling, and I'm holding him hard and he can't get away.

He twists his neck, his body. "What are you doing?"

"When the planes hit. When the towers fell. How did you feel?"

The Arab's eyes stop moving. They're always moving, moving over his candy and papers, making sure no one grabs something on the way to the subway, something for nothing. Behind his newsstand he looked taller, stronger, his neck thicker, but here on the street, no platform to stand on, he's a scared man.

"Let go of me you crazy fuck."

I lift my fist and he flinches, his head to the side, his eyes squeezed closed.

"Look at me."

"Stop this," he says.

"Pretend I'm one of the towers. Pretend you're flying the plane. Take your shot."

"Please stop," he says like a whisper, like there's not enough saliva in his mouth.

"Hit me. Take your shot."

His hands are free and I wait. Taking it will be easy. Easier than drinking. Easier than remembering. Easier than waiting for Mel. And after I take it, I'll hit what's in front of me. I'll hit until it's out of me. I'll hit and hit and hit.

I'm waiting for him and the sky's clear, another clear day, and I'm holding him under the sunlight and he doesn't do anything.

I let him go.

"Hit me," I say.

He doesn't move.

"Hit me," I say.

"Hit me," I say and I'm crying.

There are people around, standing around the newsstand. No one's saying anything. No one's doing anything. They're standing and watching. They can see he's Arab. They can see I'm American. They can guess why I'm crying.

"Hit me," I'm saying and can't get my breath.

The Arab steps back and I grab him, hold him, put my hand on his throat, press hard, harder, see his scared eyes, press harder, press until there's no choice, no choice but to hit like no choice but to jump, and his shoulder dips and his hand's a fist and I watch the punch. It doesn't hurt. Just some pressure against my head that loosens my hand. His eyes are surprised. I press my hand to his throat and there's his fist, fast.

I fall back.

I fall down.

The Arab's looking down. I feel sick. Dizzy. I blink. Blink again. He's looking down, surprised, scared. He wants to run, but he can't run. He can't run from his newsstand. He can't run from his life. I breathe into the sick feeling. I put my hands on the pavement, get myself up. I'm standing in front of him. I see the punches I'll throw. See his head snapping back. See his body on the sidewalk under me. See my fists smashing his face. Over and over and over.

I see it. But my hands aren't fists.

I see it. But I don't move forward.

I see it. But I stand still.

I take a quarter from my pocket.

I put it in his hand.

The car stops hard. The cops are out, moving to me, hands on my arms, weight pushing me down, my face against pavement, my arms pulled back, together. They stand me up. I'm facing the newsstand. Newspapers and candy cover the sidewalk. I'm pushed forward and a hand's on my head and I'm in the car and the door slams and outside the crowd is watching me.

I can smell myself like I'm someone else. I've been sweating the sweat of someone sitting and sitting and waiting, leaning against a precinct wall, head sore, body sore, thirsty, cops walking by, different cops, cuffed, transported, Central Booking, uncuffed, men's sweat, breath, piss, shit, bologna on white bread, mustard neon yellow, one bite, no place to spit, swallow, voices, snores, hours and hours, maybe the whole day, maybe the whole night. The judge is looking at papers on his desk. Garrett's standing next to me talking about me. No criminal record, a responsible citizen, an alcohol-related mistake that won't happen again. There's ink on the tips of my fingers, so black it's blue.

Garrett writes down the date, thanks the judge and I'm allowed to walk out of the room with Garrett with nothing on my wrists. He walks quickly to the elevator and we go down and through the wide lobby where people are lined in front of metal detectors waiting to get in. Going out is easy. I open the door and the sky looks morning-light and my head hurts.

Garrett's mouth is set hard and humorless. He stops at the edge of the curb and waits for the light to change. He's holding his briefcase. His shoes are perfectly parallel. "Did you have fun in there? Did you feel like a tough guy?"

I move my hand over my face. I need a shave. I feel where I've been punched.

"Do I have black on my face?"

"No," Garrett says. "The ink dries fast. They've perfected that part of the criminal justice system."

We cross Center Street. My legs are heavy like they've been fooled, like they haven't been used in days and not just one day, less than a day.

"I hope this is a wake-up call," Garrett says.

"I appreciate your help. You did well in there."

"You still have to appear in court."

"Thank you for today. I've never seen you in action. I was impressed."

"Start impressing yourself."

I leave it alone.

"You need to do something," he says. "You're drinking too much."

"I work."

"You stand still."

"It's not easy standing still. Try it and you'll see."

"I have no interest in standing still."

I stop walking. Garrett stops walking and looks at me.

"Go on," I say. "Stand still. Don't move a muscle."

"It's not a joke," he says.

"Let's get a drink."

"You're serious."

"That's what we do when we're together."

"I don't have time to drink. Some of us work more than a few hours a day. I should have been an actor and lived the life of leisure like you."

"I'm not an actor."

"Then what are you?"

Garrett's eyes are concerned, which is not what I want. I have no desire to talk, no desire to think. I want to sit in a bar, feel the weight of a glass with a fresh pour of whiskey, feel the warmth in my throat, in my stomach, alcohol spreading.

"One drink," I say. "My head hurts."

"People don't start drinking this early."

"Some people do."

Garrett makes a show of looking at his watch. It's a good watch, but not as good as The Arab's.

"Forget time," I say. "I'm thirsty."

"You're always thirsty. It's a weekday. It's a weekday morning."

"No going out on school mornings. Is that what your father told you?"

"What did your father tell you?"

"My father didn't tell me shit. Which is fine, because when people tell me things I have a hard time listening. One drink."

Garrett keeps his eyes on mine, but I can hold eyes longer than anyone, almost anyone. He moves his eyes. I look to my left and there's the gap. I see the space, the absence, the zero of Ground Zero more clearly than all the buildings there.

"Happy hour," I say.

"I'm happy enough without happy hour."

I sweep my arm across the view. "All's right with the world."

Garrett looks past my arm. Then he gets it. Almost everyone's a beat off these days. It's impossible to believe, but maybe some people don't still see what's not there.

"You're right," he says. "The world's not happy."

I put out my hand and he shakes it.

"Thank you," I say. "You helped me out."

"You're welcome."

"Really. Thank you."

"I need to tell you this. I know it's been hard for you, but as a friend I need to tell you. You're drinking too much. Beyond whatever happened yesterday, you've been drinking too much and you look beat-up."

"I look fine."

"No you don't. It really is like firewater with you. I can't deal with it sometimes. You're out of control."

"I'm in control."

"You weren't in control when you wrecked that news-stand and threatened that man. That's not some drunken night on the town. That's a hate crime. Is that how you see yourself? Are you some stupid, ignorant racist? I have a hard enough time dealing with you when you drink, but I won't deal with you at all if you keep looking for that kind of trouble."

I put my hands out, palms up, and hold them steady.

"What does that mean?" he says.

"I can still catch."

"What are you catching?"

"I'm still in control. If I have to catch, I still can catch."

I lower my hands.

"My hands are still steady," I say.

The streets are crowded. People are going to work. I look at the sky that still looks like morning, but it doesn't have to be morning. Without east or west, uptown or down-town, without two points of reference, it's hard to tell. Gar-rett opens his wallet. He takes out a business card and gives it to me. On top two upside-down Vs, a green V covering a black V.

"You have too much time on your hands," Garrett says. "That's what I think. One of my clients has a roof repair business. I asked him if he needed any workers and he said he might, so I mentioned your name. If you think it's none of my business, fine, but I asked him anyway."

"Did you tell him I'm up on assault charges?"

"They're just charges so far."

"Did you tell him I'm afraid of heights?"

"Anything else?"

"Did you tell him I'm afraid of roofs?"

I put the card in my back pocket.

"I'm going to the office," Garrett says. "I can drop you in the Village if you want."

"Go ahead. I want to walk for a while."

"You sure? You look exhausted."

"Go on."

Garrett lifts his hand to hail a cab.

"You have a court date in a month," he says. "I'm not a criminal defense attorney, but I assume I'm supposed to tell you to stay out of trouble."

"That's the line," I say.

"It's not a line. Be careful."

Garrett gets in the cab and closes the door. Then he turns to me, raises his hand, a half wave, half salute, his mouth set, concerned. The cab pulls away from the curb.

I start walking. Heavy-legged. Cold.

I hear sadness.

First it's just a tone, low and hollow, something under the words like a sluggish city breeze that keeps a discarded napkin or a stray plastic bag afloat, barely afloat, a few inches off the street. Then I hear the words, saying she misses her sister. New York City. Grief that sounds too new. Not enough alcohol to put the memories away. It all adds up.

I listen to another voice, consoling words that don't mix well with happy happy hours.

I gather the story quickly. Her sister died downtown. They haven't found her body. She wishes she could put something real in the ground, a piece even, just a piece, to visit something real in the ground.

I stay with my back to them until I hear the other one, the consoling one, excuse herself to the bathroom. I doubt she's going to look at her face in the mirror, to press cold water into her eyes, to hit something, anything.

I know what the grieving sister looks like before I turn around and I'm right, my assumption made truth, vino veritas. She has blonde hair cut just below the neck, blue eyes, fair skin that would freckle easily if it were summer, if she went to the beach, if she could be carefree. I know if she stands up from her barstool there will be something elegant in her posture without her trying, an easy comfort that comes with always being prettier than pretty enough. Her hands, open in her lap, remind me of a black and white photograph of Gandhi after he fasted for a long time and entered an altered-state of peace. For her, it must be sad acceptance, not peace. Two of her fingers are ink-stained, blue, not black. I look at the blue against her skin. Then I look at her eyes.

"Is that the best you've got?" she says and looks serious for one second, two seconds, three seconds and then she smiles so I know it's a joke. She has a sly smile, but sweet too, like her mischief would never be mean or hurtful, and only her eyes look sad.

"It is the best I've got," I say.

"No pick-up lines for you?"

"No lines. Take me or leave me. Or just look at me. I like your sad eyes."

"You like my sad eyes. I've never heard that one."

"I'm an original."

"That's a line."

"I'm a Michelangelo."

"That would be line number two."

"Two for two. And it would be wrong. These days are more like a Van Gogh. Everything isn't quite real even if it is real. I'm drinking tonight until everything gets like one of his paintings and becomes a little off. Why don't you join me?"

"Will you give me your ear?" she says.

"Tonight I will."

"And tomorrow?"

"Tomorrow you might not want my ear."

"I'm drinking Jameson," she says.

I order two shots of Jameson. I watch the bartender

pour.

"To Van Gogh," I say.

We touch glasses.

She shoots her whiskey like a pro. I wait for her eyes to narrow, for her lips to purse, even the slightest sign of a burn in her throat, but her eyes stay open and her mouth shows nothing.

"Tell me your story," I say. "I'd like to hear it."

"We're drinking to Van Gogh, remember? We're drinking to not quite real."

"Then let's have another shot."

I order two more shots. We drink them down. Her eyes and mouth stay steady.

"I lost my best friend," I say.

"I lost my sister."

"I heard you talking."

"I talk too much when I drink."

"Everyone does."

"Too much, too much," she says, joking but not, her voice exhausted, her sadness exhausting and exhausted she's been sad that long. Like fear. You get exhausted from fear and after a while, after enough time, you're too tired to feel scared the same way. I close my eyes longer than a blink and feel how tired I am, tired of anger and sadness, tired of tired. I want to feel high, at least a little. I want to feel higher than alcohol high. Sometimes Paul and I laughed so hard we couldn't stop, like two kids causing trouble in school, the teacher's stern face making it impossible to stop.

"My sister died on 9/11," she says "That's the story."

"I heard the sadness in your voice."

"Sad voice and sad eyes. I'm a lot of fun."

"He was like a brother. It's not blood. I know it's not blood, but it was close. We were very close."

"That's why we're here."

"I'm here all the time. Not here here. Just here. At some bar, somewhere."

"That's what I meant," she says.

She signals the bartender for two more shots. He pours. She lifts her glass.

"To them," she says.

We touch glasses and I watch her drink her drink straight down.

I take her hand and she lets me. Before, maybe she wasn't the kind to let a stranger in a bar take her hand, but after, now, she's tired enough to see where everything goes.

"You write," I say. "I can read that much and I haven't even looked at your palm."

"What did you look at?"

"The ink stains on your fingers."

"I'm a fact checker," she says. "For the *Daily News*."

"What facts do you check?"

"You can't tell from my hand?"

I turn her hand over and pretend to study the lines.

"No idea. I guess I'm not much of a reader after all."

"I check facts on crime stories and fill in the details if they're missing. I've only been there a year. I've only been in New York City one year. I moved here to be close to my sister, but I don't feel like leaving yet."

"Another drink?"

"Soon," she says.

I pick up my shot glass, something to do with my free hand, then put it down. Outside the bar's barred window it's still light. The days are getting longer, over the shortest-day hump.

Her friend returns from the bathroom and sits down. Her knuckles are bruise-less. We make the introductions. Her friend's name is Kathy. Her name is Sandra. I'm David. Hello. Hello. Hello.

We talk small talk. The bars and restaurants in the neighborhood. The late start for *The Sopranos* season and the arrest of its youngest star, a real-life thug in the making. The date for daylight savings.

Sandra's friend is watching me carefully. And I can see myself being careful, can feel the care in my eyes, not just a show of care. The friend says good-bye. She gives me a solid handshake. I order two more shots. Sandra downs hers, not worried about time skips with me, and I down mine, the alcohol so warm, so smooth, it's almost a moat against the world. One of her hands is still open on her lap.

"My sister was in Tower Two."

"My friend was in Tower One."

"What do I do?" she says.

"What do I do?" she says again.

Repetitions all over the place. Of falling towers. Of grief.

Of little-man acts. Of drinking. Drinking and drinking.

"Are you drunk?"

"I'm drunk," she says.

"Good. I'm drunk too."

"Good," she says.

She tucks her hair behind her ear.

"I can't read your hands," she says. "What do you do?"

I hold my hands out, keep them steady.

"This," I say.

"What?"

"I stand very still and don't move."

"What does that mean?"

"Come with me," I say.

She stands elegantly like I knew she would and puts on her coat and we walk out of the bar.

We walk downtown. It just happens that way. I don't know where she lives, but I know it's downtown.

We wake and sleep, half wake, half sleep, sweating out our hangovers, and after the garbage trucks make their wake-up calls, trash compactor moans that build to a crescendo and then diminish down the street, we sleep for hours straight. We both dream but can't remember our dreams. Sandra calls in sick to work.

"Crime will have to take a break today," she says.

"Is that all it takes?"

"If they don't print the story, what's the point in committing the crime?"

"No glory."

"It's almost true. You'd be surprised how many convicted felons contact the paper to tell their stories all over again. A clipping about what they did, or how they almost got away makes their fifteen minutes of infamy official."

"I'll remember that."

"What crime are you committing?"

"When I tell you, make me look good."

Sandra puts her head on my chest, drapes her arm across my stomach. I'm looking at the ceiling.

"The high of their lives," I say. "Their movie-star moment. If they could trade their high to get out of prison, I wonder what they'd choose. Freedom or the high."

"It's not a movie."

"Their high must be like a movie, or at least their memory of the high."

"Have you ever been to prison?"

"Not yet." I blur my eyes and the lines in the ceiling go away. Then I focus my eyes and the lines come back. "There was a time I treated everything like a movie. I would have been acting even while the cops were chasing me."

"What time was that?"

"When I had Hollywood in my eyes."

"And now?"

"You've seen my eyes. They're just eyes."

"I like your eyes," she says.

"I could have been a contender."

Sandra adjusts her head and I feel her relax into me. Her hair's soft against my skin.

"I could stay like this all day," she says.

"It's your sick day. You can do whatever you want. I can call in sick too."

"We'll both be sick."

Sandra puts her hand against my forehead like she's feeling for fever.

"Will I live?"

"You'll live," she says. "So what should we do on our sick day?"

"We can stay in bed. We can get something to eat. We can take a walk and wander the streets."

"Do you walk a lot?"

"I used to walk a lot when I first moved here. Now I run more than walk, but I think I've walked every street in this city. It's still surprising sometimes. Even now something will pull my attention and I'll see a building or a store or some sign or a painted doorway I've never seen before."

"New York is that big."

"Usually I see things I have seen before. Almost every street has a memory."

"Let's take a walk. You can show me some of your memories and I'll show you some of mine."

"Now they're almost all connected to that day."

She takes her head off my chest to look at me.

"Me too," she says. "It's almost worse when I remember something nice or fun. I'll remember and then that day comes in."

"It's everywhere."

"It's everywhere here."

"Maybe we should stay in."

"It's here too. We're talking about it."

"Maybe we should drink. Every time I walk out of a subway station, I'll look up at the buildings and the sky and remember."

"I imagine planes flying too low all the time."

"I keep thinking buildings are going to fall."

"I hate loud noises. I hate sirens."

"I keep looking toward the hole."

"You know what I want? I want that day to stop attaching itself to my memories of my sister. It's like cancer. A person gets cancer and all you remember is the person has cancer. They're stigmatized for life and then for death. I don't want that for my sister."

She puts her head back on my chest and I move my hand through her hair. We listen to the city sounds. I bring her to me and we kiss, slow kissing, like this one day off from work will last. I move my mouth over her neck, over her shoulder, over her. I listen to the sounds she makes, quiet sounds, almost like she's quietly crying. I move my body on top of her body, move inside her.

"Be right now," I say.

I want the now to be real. I want the now to be now.

"Now," she says.

Now and now and now and Mel comes in.

She sleeps.

She wakes.

We dress without showering, two bums for the day, smelling of sex and cooled sweat. It's March-bright outside and cold but softer cold, which comes when days get longer, which can't be measured by temperature. We walk the Village streets, our shared neighborhood. We point to buildings and intersections and subway stops and talk about city memories, all of them before.

We're walking past the bar and I think about keeping quiet, but stop.

"This is where I went right after. I sat here with everyone else sitting here. I stared at the TV. And I drank. I drank and drank."

Sandra is looking at the bar, changing what she sees to a clear September day almost six months ago.

"Do you still drink and drink?"

"You met me drinking."

"I was drinking too, but usually I don't drink so much."

"I usually do."

"I tried to go downtown," she says. "I tried to get as far downtown as I could, but I couldn't get very far. I started making calls from my cell phone, but none of them went through. I went home and started making calls from my phone there and I still couldn't get through. I went to my office. I thought their phones might work better. They were news phones, so I thought they might work, but they didn't, at least not at first. I finally got through to my parents. They told me they hadn't heard from her either. When the lines opened up, my phone would ring and I'd pray before I looked at the number. All that's left to hear is if they find her body or not, but I don't think they'll find many more bodies."

"They haven't found Paul."

"Paul. You didn't say his name until now."

"That's his name."

"My sister's name is Sharon."

We start walking again.

"Hey," she says.

"What?"

"You're supposed to say it's a nice name."

"It is a nice name."

"I'm teasing."

"Sandra and Sharon."

"David and Paul."

"David and Paul," I say and it's the first time I've ever said our names out loud like that. I don't say the third name out loud.

"What was the last thing you said to each other?" she says.

"Nothing nice."

"No."

"Paul and I had a fight before it happened."

"I'm sorry."

"Bad timing," I say.

She waits. And I decide to talk. To not be so careful. To not make him precious in the worst way.

"We had a fight and didn't talk for months. He'd call, but I wouldn't answer the phone. He'd leave messages and joke about how I wasn't speaking to him. Then he left messages just asking me to call him back. I'd listen to him talking into the machine, but I wouldn't pick up. He even wrote me a letter. And then too much time passed. And then he was dead."

"What did you fight about?"

"He didn't like how I was living my life."

"Did you like how you were living your life?"

We're walking the streets, New York City, the center of the world, but these streets are our neighborhood, just like any neighborhood, a supermarket, a drug store, a laundromat, a shoe-repair shop, places to take care of necessities.

"After he got married he judged me more. He was happy with his wife and he wanted me to have that kind of happiness. Paul felt I was just going through the motions and playing parts beyond the parts I played when I was acting and that I needed something more. I didn't like my life, but that's how I was living it. I didn't like him telling me what to do or not do. I didn't like being pushed. We had it out and I stopped talking to him and then he was dead. Just like that."

It's March bright and softer cold and maybe we should drink.

"I started seeing someone a month before it happened,

so I sacrificed time with her. That's natural, that's what happens when you start seeing someone, and she was happy for me, but now I wish I'd spent more time with my sister. I almost wish I'd never met him. I didn't know she'd be gone all of a sudden."

"I don't think Paul regretted anything in his life."

"That's a good way to live."

"It's impossible to know, but I don't think he did. Even with his job. Everyone assumes Wall Street is about trading in your time to get rich, but for him it was more. He liked putting together complicated deals and he liked most of the people he worked with and he never let work take over his life. If he worked a ridiculously long day, he'd make sure to go out afterward, and when he finished a big project, he'd take a three-day weekend and do whatever he felt like doing. He lived. He traveled. I didn't really travel until I met Paul. And he had a wild streak, but not mean wild. He did what he wanted in a good way, a fun way. It didn't make sense to him to do something he didn't really want to do. My life didn't make sense to him. Fuck it. Now nothing makes sense, so it doesn't matter."

"Sense will come back."

"Maybe it shouldn't."

"In a civilized world, sense comes back."

"A civilized world? There's no such thing."

"I think there is. Look around. People are going about their lives."

"Fly a plane into a building and the veneer will crack."

"And it will return. I think it's more solid than a veneer."

Her face is almost a kid's face, symmetrical, even spaces between her eyes and nose and mouth. Only the lines around her eyes, grief lines, show she's lived.

"Tell me some more about Paul," she says.

"See that pizza place? Sometimes we'd end our nights there. He liked their Sicilian slices. He always asked for a corner piece."

"What else?"

"And a Coke."

"Tell me."

"Okay. What else. He was an optimistic person, but he wasn't stupid about it and it wasn't because he was blind. Paul's optimism was effortless. When he was having fun it was genuine fun. That's why it was so great to travel with him. We went to Europe and we drove across country and when I looked at new places through his eyes, they really looked new. Even New York looked new through his eyes. But we didn't live the same life here most of the time. I was looking through my eyes. He thought I was too moody, like I was some fake James Dean who thought being moody would help me make it. Paul didn't play any parts. He felt things didn't have to be so dark to be romantic. He felt life didn't have to be so dark. Maybe he was wrong. These days are dead."

A dog barks. Another dog barks in return. Without leashes the barks could lead to more than barking.

"So you play a lot of parts?" she says.

"According to Paul I was always playing. The bullshit romantic. The pretend tough-guy."

"And that made you angry at him."

"I didn't want to hear it."

"Was he right?"

"I've thought I've known people. I've been wrong."

"That happens sometimes," she says. "That's allowed."

We've circled around. We're back near Father Demo Square.

"I'm going to walk you home."

"That's too easy," she says.

"I've heard that too."

She looks at me and looks away. Her hands are in her coat pockets.

"Too easy," I say.

The sidewalk looks clean in the sun. She pulls her hair from her eyes, tucks it behind her ear.

"Sometimes I do the easy thing," I say.

She doesn't react. Like downing a shot. Like she's tough enough to take anything.

We walk.

"Let's get something to eat," I say. "You need your strength."

"Why?"

"You're sick today, remember? We're both sick."

"I forgot."

"What are you in the mood for?"

"You haven't called in sick yet."

"Give me your phone."

I call the school. The receptionist doesn't know me. There's a long list of nude models. She says she'll pass the message along.

"It's official," I say. "I'm sick."

"We're both sick."

I give Sandra her phone.

We get egg sandwiches from the bodega and sit on a bench in Father Demo Square, the square where I sat that morning. I don't tell her. She eats well, with real appetite. Mel didn't eat well. But maybe she's eating in France. Maybe her appetite came back.

Blast. Adrenaline. Then recognition. Not terrorism. Just a car, backfire echoing against concrete. The pigeons have lifted off, flying one way, flying the other way and then they fly up, higher than the bell tower of Our Lady of Pompeii, its stained glass windows and stone façade out of place and time.

"I want to walk some more," she says.

We walk uptown on Seventh Avenue.

I watch the cars driving south.

St. Vincent's is across the avenue, square and solid as if the building itself could give faith to the sick inside. Sandra stops, takes my hand and we cross. We walk up the stairs to the wall with all the faces. Photograph. Name. Date of birth. Physical description. Employer. Tower number. Floor number. MISSING.

Sandra guides me along the wall and stops. She points

to a face like her own, a woman with blond hair, prettier than just pretty.

"I come here almost every day," Sandra says.

There's nothing to say so I don't say anything.

I run.

I stand.

I sleep.

I don't get a postcard from Mel. TOO MUCH SUN. ONE PICTURE PER PLACE. Seven words from weeks ago, weeks of too much sun. Maybe she's used to it now. Maybe it's not too much anymore. I tell Paul I won't stop. I won't stop waiting for Mel.

"Just for fun," she says.

"Just for fun."

"Okay, just."

"You'll be late for work."

"It's not like I punch a clock," Sandra says.

She sips her coffee. I fork a half-slice of toast, pick it off the plate, take a bite.

"This was my movie-star move. If I ever did a breakfast scene, this is what I'd do. In the movie, I'd be disheveled from a hard night out, hungover, but feeling good too, to be awake, to be with this new woman I'd just met and liked and we'd be eating breakfast in a diner and I'd fork a piece of toast like this instead of picking it up with my hand. It would be one of those bullshit method-actor moves, quirky and pointless, that people remember."

"Very impressive," she says, smiling.

"I won't be able to do the toast move at the audition."

"Why not?"

"I'm not hungover. Plus they don't provide real forks for the actors. It doesn't look the same when you have to pretend-fork something."

"We can borrow one of these forks."

"Borrow?"

"I'll return it."

"I'm happy to steal a fork, but let's play hooky instead. We'll go to a bar. I'll order us a couple shots of Jameson. I was impressed with your poker face when I met you. It was a good move, downing whiskey like a tough guy. You can do a repeat performance."

"Repeat performances rarely turn out the same. Go to the audition and see how it is."

"Just for fun."

"For fun and not just for fun. Because it's something you did before."

"Maybe I didn't want to do it before. Maybe I just did it."

I fork my toast.

"See," she says. "You still have your moves."

"Look at me."

She finishes her coffee. I drink the rest of my water. I put down a tip, pay the bill and we're outside the diner. The light changes and we cross Sixth Avenue.

"Hold on," she says. "I wouldn't want someone mistaking me for an actor."

She takes out the copy of *Backstage* from her bag. She takes out my picture and resume that she asked me to bring over, that she wanted to see, just curious. I didn't say anything when I saw *Backstage* on her kitchen table opened to the audition she'd already circled in blue pen, the same blue that smudges her fingers. I could have been angry. I could have told her to let me do what I had to do, or not do what I didn't have to do.

"Here," she says.

I take the paper and my picture.

"What?" she says.

"Paul didn't want me to act anymore."

"In life or like this?"

"You'll see when we get there."

"Did he act?"

"He never auditioned. He had no interest in making it. He didn't need to make it, so he didn't know."

I haven't bought *Backstage* in months. I haven't auditioned in months. The audition's in the neighborhood, at NYU's film school, the listing for a character I can play, my body, my coloring, my type, summed up in a sentence as if a person could be distilled. She's in France, hard rocks on the beach, too much sun, with The Arab who's more than a type.

"So what exactly do you do at an audition?" she says.

"You pretend you're someone else."

West 4th is empty. It looks like Sunday morning.

"This one's for a film," I say. "So they give you sides. A few pages with lines of dialogue. You go into a room and you read the sides for the camera and then you leave the room. The trick is to make the lines real."

"It's a trick?"

"My mistake. It's a technique."

"I wouldn't be good at that," Sandra says. "I'd have to stop and check the facts. I'd have to make sure all the lines were true."

We walk past the law school, the courtyard in front a quiet haven to sit and think. The benches are empty. A pigeon stands just inside the gate, cleaning its feathers, head swiveled, a purple sheen to its chest like spilled gasoline in the sun.

"When do they let you know if you got the part or not?"

"It depends on the audition. I learned a long time ago not to wait by the phone."

"That has to be hard."

We're walking too fast, like we need to get there. I slow the pace. The NYU flag, emblazoned with a torch, hangs above the Tisch School, but this part of Broadway isn't lit like uptown.

"How do I look?"

I pull my hand through my hair, squint my eyes, tough James Dean, then cross them. She smiles, what I wanted.

"Perfect," she says. "I'd cast you in a heartbeat."

"And action."

I open the door.

The guard checks our IDs and tells us to sign the sign-in sheet attached officially to a clipboard. He doesn't frisk us. He doesn't look through Sandra's bag. He's like a bad actor emoting security.

We take the elevator up. There's a real actor in the elevator, easy to spot. When he introduces himself to the director he'll over enunciate his name, then deliver his lines like it's opening night on Broadway, not a moment on film where a narrowed eye can show everything. But maybe I'm wrong. Maybe he's better than that. And that's fine. I used to put myself against all of them, strut into an audition like I already had the part, look them down when they looked too long. It kept me alone, away from pre-audition talk and pre-audition fear. I had to make it. I had to win. I look at Sandra looking at the numbers going up. The elevator door opens. The actor's out first.

"There's no point," I say.

"We're here."

We walk the hall, find the room, door closed, table outside, copies of sides in neat piles. The pages are more space than typed words. Bold letters highlight camera angles. It's the barest blueprint for a movie shoot.

A young woman, college-aged, wearing retro glasses, is

signing people in. I open my wallet and show her my SAG card.

"Will this help me cut the line?"

"It will," the woman says and puts a check by my name.

I give her my picture and resume. She gives me sides for the character Sandra circled. I put my hand on Sandra's shoulder.

"Good job."

"I've got you pegged," she says.

Folding chairs line the hall. We sit near the end of the line and I hold the pages so Sandra can see them too.

"It's a great scene. Maybe the greatest."

"Just for fun," she says.

"It's not for fun. It's me against them. That's how I always approached it."

"Why?"

"Because that's what it is."

"Isn't acting supposed to be collaborative?"

"Not at an audition. Not until the movie's cast."

"If I were auditioning, I think I'd pretend we were all in the movie together."

"I have other things to pretend."

I look at all the actors. I read the scene again. The man's talking to the woman he lives with. She's upset her brother lost his job at the fire department. He's upset his car was stolen. She's upset he's not listening to her. He's upset her family runs her life. Easy motivations and emotions, escalating easily. It's no surprise the camera follows him storming out of the apartment. Their word. Storming.

"The trick is to figure out how to storm."

"That must require advanced technique," she says.

"Do the facts line up?"

"Completely."

"I'll make them real."

"What do you do right before you start speaking?"

"I look at the camera and wink."

"Tell me."

"I whisper the character's name like it's my own."

"David," she says in a whisper.

"That's too loud. And you shouldn't be playing me."

Two actors leave the audition room. They don't look happy. They almost never look happy, but at least then they look real. If I were casting people I'd catch them on the way out, when they were done trying too hard, tell them that now the real audition was starting. The woman at the table calls two more names. Two actors stand, a leading man, a leading woman, and walk into the audition room.

"It's like a doctor's office for good-looking couples," Sandra says.

I read the lines once more.

"Do you want to go in with me?"

"No," she says.

"I'll ask them. I'll ask if you can."

"That's okay."

"All this planning and you came to sit in the hall and wait?"

She doesn't say anything.

"You could have waited outside the diner. I could have walked in the door and walked back out the door. That could have been your collaborative effort. I'd walk in, I'd walk out, and you'd watch. We didn't need to come here for that."

Sandra doesn't move her eyes, but she covered better downing shots of Jameson.

"There's no point," I say.

The two actors leave the room. The proctor calls two more names. Sandra takes a copy of yesterday's *News* from her bag and turns the pages. Maybe she's checking facts she already checked.

"They stole my car," I say.

She looks up and my eyes aren't so hard, I know my eyes, know how they'd look stretched across a screen, and she smiles. "That sounded real."

"My Valiant. My Plymouth Valiant. I put so many hours of work into that car. You can't find cars like that anymore."

"What color?"

"Green. Light green."

Two actors leave the room. The proctor calls my name and another name and a woman a few chairs down stands. I look at Sandra.

"Last chance," I say.

"They stole your car," she says.

I walk to the door and let the woman through first. In the room, a man stands behind a camera mounted on a tripod. Another man sits behind a desk looking over 8 by 10s. I've done this too many times. Read. Read again at callbacks. Sometimes cast. But I never got the part where I could fork a piece of toast. I never got the part that would put me in the book of photos I'd looked at as a kid. I'd turn the pages slow. I'd turn the pages fast, all the faces moving like a movie, one movie star moving into the next. A picture in a book. A moment forking a half-slice of toast. Paul telling me it's not enough, not for me, telling me for me. I can leave right now, go to the table, take back my picture, not look at the camera, walk out of the room. Like a doctor's appointment you just decide to leave. Even in his office, even while the exam is happening, fingers probing, you can still leave. You can pull the needle from your arm. They can't make you stay, can't make you take it. Sandra's outside. It's just an audition. It's just pretend. I can just stay, just read with the other actor, just see how it feels, and then we'll be done and I'll let her leave the room first, then me.

We sit on the two chairs set up in front of the camera. I look at the woman. I make her Sandra. I didn't fight him, but I faced him, an LA fireman with clear eyes. I make him her brother.

The director's looking at our pictures, not us. "Say your names into the camera and begin the scene when you're ready."

She says her name. I say mine.

I look at the woman across from me and her eyes go from calm to hard and her mouth tightens. She's upset about her brother. I'm upset about my stolen Valiant. She's upset with me. We read through the sides, talking to each other. I'm listening to her and she's listening to me and we run out of lines.

The director puts our pictures on a pile of pictures. He thanks us for reading and says he'll be contacting people for callbacks at the end of the week.

We walk out and I close the door. Sandra's reading her paper, but I can't tell if her eyes are on the words, or if they're far away. Sometimes she looks like she's looking, but she's not. I've seen it in Mel, a residual of grief, an almost-blank stare that's really a wish for a blank stare, the peace of seeing nothing, a good nothing, but they're both seeing too much. Sometimes, when I see their eyes like that, I try to bring them back, fast, like waking someone from a nightmare. You hear the moan, feel the shudder. It's fascinating, not knowing what they're seeing, just knowing it's not good. But not waking them immediately is irresponsibly cruel. I touch her shoulder as fast as I can. Sandra looks up.

"Hi. I'm done. Let's go."

We walk to the elevator, the door opens, actors come out, we go in. The two of us are closest to the door and in the closed door's reflection I see her and me and everyone else is background. The door opens and what's outside replaces our reflections, the real lobby and the real people in the lobby waiting for the elevator and we're out, through the lobby, outside. Sandra waits for me to talk.

"You want the long version or the short?"

"Whatever version you prefer."

"If I hadn't read well, I wouldn't trust what I don't feel."

"What don't you feel?" she says.

"I don't need it. Or I don't need it right now. Without resentment or doubt. I didn't need it in there. That's the short version."

"I couldn't hear you with the door closed," she says. "But I can tell you're good."

"You saw me forking toast."

"If I saw you forking toast in a film, I'd remember the moment."

"B movies. Cigarette moves. I used to dream of A-list Hollywood."

East Broadway's crowded. Cars. Shoppers. The downtown crowd starting their day late, going somewhere.

"I used to take classes, I used to work hard at it and for a while I wanted to be good. I wanted to be better than good. Then it became about making it. It was always about making it, but then that's all it became. And then Paul was right. I wasn't living life."

I'm not yelling. I'm not running. She waits, listening, but I don't have anything else to say and I'm aware of the noise, the volume turned up, traffic, horns, people talking, and a truck shifts gear, loud, taking all the other noise, and the light changes and we walk.

"The big decisions come to me," she says. "When I have to decide something big, I force myself not to think about it. I know my mind will work on its own, through whatever it is, and then I'll know what to do."

"I don't want to think," I say.

"Then don't."

"Amazing. That's amazing. It works."

"You have a nice smile when you smile," she says.

We cross the street. She stops walking. We're standing in front of the subway steps.

"Now what?"

"Now I need to go to work," she says.

She smiles a different smile, like she's known me a long time.

Sandra tucks her hair behind her ear. I don't watch her walk down the steps.

I get a postcard from Mel. The same postcard.

ONE PLACE. SO ONE PICTURE. STILL.

She doesn't sign her name to this card either. If she signed her name she'd have to sign other words. *Sincerely*. She'd laugh at that. *Fondly*. She'd laugh at that too, the formality of it all. *Love*. She couldn't sign it love. He's here, but he's not.

Sandra stops in the stationery store to buy two pens. We go to Trattoria de Pesce to eat. She orders a glass of red wine and I get a beer, Moretti, the cartoon man on the label hoisting a stein, fedora on his head, too-thick moustache. Halfway through the beer I want a bourbon, want many bourbons, no cartoons on the bottle.

The busboy clears our plates. The waiter recites the list of desserts, prefacing each selection with *We have a nice*. We decide to share a piece of *we have a nice* chocolate mousse cake.

"I have some news," she says. "The paper offered me a small byline. Beat stuff, local crime, the kind of stuff I was fact checking."

"That's great. Congratulations."

"Thank you," she says.

"We have a nice robbery. We have a nice assault. We have a nice embezzlement. We have a nice drug sale." I make sure to leave off the crimes of hijacking, mass murder and terrorism.

The busboy walks by, his arm stacked with plates. He wears a red vest perfect for tomato sauce stains.

The waiter places the piece of cake between us and sets down two forks. Sandra forks off a piece of cake. Her fingers are stained where they're always stained.

"Will you get as much ink on your fingers with your new position?"

"Probably. I like to write by hand."

She eats a piece of cake. I eat a piece of cake.

"It doesn't feel like New York right now," she says.

"What does it feel like?"

"I don't know. It feels like we're away somewhere."

"Somewhere nice?"

"Somewhere nice. We have a nice destination. It doesn't happen a lot, but sometimes when I'm with you I feel we're somewhere else. I don't think you feel that way, but I do. Usually I look at people who didn't lose someone like they're a different species. They have their dinners and their weekends and the details of their lives and they're far away, but sometimes when we're together I feel far away like them. For hours at a time I almost forget."

"Have some more cake."

"New York City," she says.

"It's starting to look like a parking lot down there."

"They're cleaning things up."

"Clean," I say.

"They were so tall they hardly seemed real when I looked up at them. It was the same thing on top. My sister and I went up to the observation deck one night to see the view and it looked as unreal looking down."

"When the planes hit, that looked the most unreal of all."

Sandra moves her fork through the cake but doesn't pick up the piece.

"Can you remember them?" she says. "I mean, can you remember them exactly as they were?"

"Every time I look downtown I see the towers."

"Every time?" she says.

She's watching me for a lie.

"No," I say. "Not every time. You're right. I don't see them every time. I see the towers most of the time but not always. Sometimes I look downtown and for a moment, for a first moment before I remember, it looks like there was never anything there."

"That's what happens with time."

"I hate it."

"Sometimes I hate it," she says.

"Even a day later, even that afternoon, I heard people talking like nothing had happened. I walked miles that day and the farther uptown I got, the less people seemed to care. Even their faces didn't look the same as the people's faces downtown. I passed two guys talking and one of them actually said what a beautiful day it was. There wasn't any irony in his voice. He wasn't talking about how fucked up it was to have good weather that day. He was talking about the weather like that was all there was to say. And that was the day it happened."

"That was wrong."

"That was more than wrong. And now it's more than wrong. Everyone's homogenizing everything. They're talking about the good that came out of this and about how New Yorkers came together and how polite the city became. But no one's talking about the people who lost someone, who don't know what to do with themselves, who go on living but not really. It's the not really. They don't know the not really. New York's so big it's covering up the loss, but you can't cover the loss if you lost someone. And no one's really talking about making amends. People were killed and nothing's being done."

"There's not much to do. It was a suicide mission."

"I'm angry all the time. I'm sad all the time too, but I'm angry and I don't know where to put it."

"I don't either."

"And sometimes I'm more tired than angry. Maybe that's good. Maybe that's weak. I don't know."

"Tired's not weak."

She's holding her fork but not using it.

"Were you angry before?" she says.

"Before. That's just how I say it. Before. There's before. There's after. Christ is no longer the line. Before the World Trade Center. After the World Trade Center. BWTC and AWTC. The new demarcation of time."

Her eyes go away to before, to when the towers stood, maybe to when she went with her sister to the top and they looked at Manhattan spread before them, lit up at night, and then her eyes come back, after.

"Were you?" she says. "Were you so angry before?"

"I was careless before. I treated people carelessly. My dreams were all about me and I wasn't as successful as I thought I should be and that made me angry. I knew the world owed me nothing, but I was still angry. But it was petty anger. I probably knew that even then. Now I have something to be angry about. They killed my friend."

"I'm angry too," she says.

"But you're forgiving."

"I'm angry at them for what they did, the terrorists, the nebulous terrorists, but I want to believe the world is basically good. I hope I'll believe again what I believed before."

"What do you believe right now?"

"Right now I'm eating chocolate cake."

"Someone I know told me if you pretend hard enough, eventually you won't have to pretend at all. I don't know if I believe it."

"Was the person an actor?"

"No."

She points to the cake with her fork. "It's your turn."

"Pretend," I say. "I don't even like the word anymore."

"Then don't pretend."

"The world is basically good. It's pretend. You're pretending."

"I'm sorry you feel that way," she says. "That's your prerogative, but I don't think I'm pretending. There are good people in the world and that makes it good. My sister was good. Your friend Paul sounds like he was good. I think you're good."

"Paul wanted me to be a better man for a reason."

"A better man. That doesn't mean you're not a good man."

"I look at my hands sometimes and they're fists."

"I've seen your hands. I hope that feeling will pass."

"I don't know if I want it to pass. When I feel it passing I walk over to Sixth Avenue and glance downtown and it all comes back."

I fork off some cake and push the plate to her. She finishes the last piece.

"I see the dark part of humanity all the time," she says. "Some of the crimes we cover are barbaric, but it's mostly about the where and the when and the how. Lately I try to think about the why."

"The why is because men are dark and selfish and hateful. That's the why. You can justify as much as you want, but it's true."

"There are reasons people do what they do."

"I could blame everything I do on my past, but that's too easy. My friend is dead. Your sister is dead."

"Yes they are."

"I was out with some people, some Arabs and some Americans, and one of the Americans got angry and started talking about how the Arabs danced as soon as the towers came down."

"Some of them danced."

"I know that. I know the news stations played the same shots over and over that day. I know only a few people celebrated. And when this man started going off on how we should bomb all of them, bomb them all to hell, it sounded ugly. But I understood how he felt. I didn't say anything. But then I did something."

"What did you do?"

"Nothing I'm proud of doing. But some of them did dance."

"There were small pockets of hate. If you read the papers, there were thousands of vigils all over the world, including the Middle East. Most of the world was mourning with us."

She picks up her fork, presses it against the plate, smudges some leftover icing. "From working at the paper I've learned that most violent crimes are reactions. They're not about hate. Sometimes they're long-term reactions, but they're still reactions. What happened here was a reaction to things we did."

"We never flew planes into their buildings."

"We did other things."

"We didn't do that."

"No we didn't, but we did do other things."

The busboy carries plates to the back.

"I walked away from Paul."

"I know."

"I ran away from Paul."

"I know."

"Even if I wanted to run back I can't and part of me hates him for that. Maybe I would have run back, but maybe I wouldn't have. And now it's too late. I didn't run back and he's dead and my hands are fists all the time."

She's holding her fork. Her hand is so steady the fork doesn't move, but the not-moving seems more sad than peaceful.

"I think you would have gone back eventually," she says.

"That's pretend. You don't know."

"I'm not pretending."

We sit quiet.

Sandra looks past me at the other diners.

I signal for the check and we leave.

We walk the West Village streets. I look into the bars we pass.

The big police van is parked on the south side of Washington Square. They're still watching the drug dealers, who still work the park.

"You should write about that," I say. "It's like a child's game. After everything that's gone on, they worry about ten-dollar marijuana sales."

"That's not a bad idea."

"It's a nice idea."

"It's a nice idea," she says and the smile's in her voice. "Maybe I should get you a job at the paper."

A runner passes us, legs kicking high like my stride when I run, doing laps of the square.

"Sunday night," she says. "I have a busy week ahead."

"*The party's over.*"

"*All things must come to an end.* I know that song."

"My father used to sing that all the time. Whenever he broke up with a woman he'd sing that song, but the way he sang it the words sounded happy. *The party's over.* I came to New York as soon as I could."

"Here we are," she says.

"Me and you and the drug dealers."

"And the police playing a child's game."

"And the dogs in the dog run."

She takes my hand, squeezes once to let me know, to let the now be now. It's something Paul might have done if he'd held my hand.

With the trees and the quiet and the buildings low to the ground and the Washington Square arch cutting off the high-rises on both sides so it's only the stretch of Fifth Avenue ahead, downtown feels far away.

"Sometimes."

"Sometimes what?" she says.

"It almost feels like before."

"It does," she says. "Sometimes. And that's not bad."

We walk west on West 4th Street. Kids hang out in front of the tattoo parlors, stretching the weekend as far as they can.

"Do you want to spend the night?" she says.

"We have a nice night," I say like the waiter and she smiles. But there's after in her smile, in her smile and the way she looks straight ahead.

"You don't have to," she says.

"I know."

"You don't."

"*You said it already, George.*"

"Who's George?"

"When Paul and I were in London, two guys were hawking sets of dishes on the street. There was a big crowd around them and a big stack of dishes in front of them. One guy was doing all the talking about the quality of the dishes and their durability and their beautiful design and the other guy just stood next to him, silently nodding his head. The first guy talked on and on, hawking away, practically caressing the dishes, building up their worth, but it was all a set-up, and the entertaining thing was how blatant the set-up was, how you knew he was holding the moment before he revealed the bottom line, the bottom line everyone was waiting for, which was the cost of the dishes. He kept talking and everyone kept waiting and all of a sudden the other guy, the silent guy, blurted out the price. The first guy made this horrified face, like his buddy had just made the biggest mistake in the world, like the price he'd blurted out was so ridiculously low it was criminal. Then the hawker raised his hands, his face moving from horror to disgust to resignation, and he yelled at his friend for the whole crowd to hear, *You said it already, George. You said it already*. And that was the price. That was the price they sold the dishes for, a bargain for all those lucky enough to hear George's stupid mistake. People actually stepped up and started buying boxes of those dishes. They were a good team. And you could tell the hawker enjoyed creating all that build-up and the other guy enjoyed waiting for the perfect moment to blurt out the price. You could tell it was a show, but it wasn't just a show because the two of them were having fun."

"*You said it already, George*," she says.

"*You said it already*. It's a good line."

We cross Seventh Avenue.

I squeeze her hand.

"Yes. I'd like to spend the night."

"Good," she says. "Let's go home."

I don't say anything, not about her word home, not about us going home. It has a nice sound to it, if nothing else.

We walk to her apartment. We go up and get undressed. She sets the alarm. She turns off the lights. We get into bed. Her body is warm, her hands warm on my back, but I'm not all here.

A plane moves across the sky, higher than any building, its engines louder than the traffic, and I watch until a building obstructs my view. She's a plane ride away. A night in the air, then the sun rising horizon-less, a different kind of time skip. I see her meeting me at the airport. I'm coming off the plane and she's there. If she were flying here, she wouldn't be here yet. European flights land late at Kennedy, late afternoon and evening. But I'd go to the airport now, maybe make a sign bigger than a postcard and hold it up when she came. Bold letters. MEL. Maybe underneath I'M HERE.

I run.

I stand.

I sleep.

I wait for Mel.

I see it like it's real. I'm in prison, in my cell, sitting and staring. I eat with men. I walk the yard with men. I shower with men. I shit with men. I'm standing in front of a brick building on Columbus Avenue and I punch like I can take it, like I can do whatever I have to do and I look at my hand. Two skinned knuckles. Some blood. A checklist of little damages. I flex my hand. I can still catch.

The sign outside says Happy Hour. The sign outside says Oysters for a Dollar. There are people inside drinking and eating oysters.

The bar is light and long and I order one drink and a second and it's warm. I look at my hand. No oysters in prison. I let myself feel the fear as if it's real, as if it will happen.

There's a very fat man on my left trying too hard to talk to two women. There's a couple on my right, asking each other first-date questions. The bartender's filling two pint glasses with Guinness. When the bartender looks up I order another bourbon and a dozen oysters.

There's no clock here. I don't know if there are clocks there. Doing time. If you do half your time, the second half is faster. That's the way with everything. The second half always moves.

The bartender puts down the plate of oysters and I

squeeze lemon and take one, taste sea, taste salt.

The fat man turns to me. His face is pig-like, his eyes squinty from puffed cheeks. He's too pale. His heart, struggling all the time, has to be tired.

"How are the oysters in this place?"

"The first one tasted good to me."

"They look fresh."

"Have one if you like."

"Really?"

"I'm feeling generous."

"Thank you," he says.

He takes the oyster in his thick fingers, places the shell in his mouth and sucks down the meat with joy.

"So how are the oysters in this place?"

"Not bad," he says. "Not bad at all. I've eaten oysters from the cold waters of Maine to Apalachicola, which is on the Gulf Coast, to the coast of Alaska where I always order Olympia oysters. Olympias are dwindling in numbers, unfortunately, but they're delicious and worth the price."

"An oyster aficionado."

"If there is such a thing. What happened to your hand?"

"I punched a wall."

"A wall puncher," he says. "I've seen a lot of those."

"Are you saying I'm a type?"

The fat man's not sure how to answer. I can see him deciding whether to say something smart, or ignore what I've said, or turn back to the two women who've given him nothing. The alcohol's in me and I can see everything.

"I've seen hands like that on fighters," he says.

"Are you in the fight business?"

"I worked in the ER when I did my residency. The hospital was near a boxing gym, so I saw a lot of broken hands."

"I fight walls and I lose."

"Poor anger management?"

"Only when I drink. So watch out."

The fat man stares at me, then his face relaxes and his eyes don't look so pressed.

"Are you free tonight?" he says.

"Free," I say and smile.

"Are you?"

"It depends on the plan."

"Here's the plan," the fat man says. "Dinner is on me if you can get these two women to go out with us. I'll throw in a room at The Plaza if you can get them back to the hotel."

"Is that where you're staying?"

"I always stay at The Plaza when I'm in New York City. It reminds me of another time."

"Why not pick them up yourself? Flash them some cash, rich man."

"I don't like doing that."

"Then just talk. See where it goes naturally."

"Have you looked at me? I could speak like Shakespeare and it wouldn't matter."

"If you spoke like Shakespeare, you could bed those two."

"Unfortunately I don't. Like most women I meet, they

keep looking around whenever I talk to them, hoping no one will think they're with me."

"So that's the challenge."

"It's not a challenge. It's an impossibility. Are you up for my challenge?"

"I'm done with challenges."

"Then let me impose on you," he says.

"Can you see me in prison?"

"Have you ever been?"

"Never. But can you see me there?"

The fat man stares again. His eyes, more open now, are kind.

"No," he says. "I can't see you in prison. Not even with a banged-up hand."

I take an oyster, suck it down.

"Well?" the fat man says. "Will you help me out?"

I signal the bartender for another drink.

"It's on his tab," I say.

The bartender pours, I drink, two quick gulps.

I lean over the bar, look straight at the women. They're talking, intent, something about work, a change of offices, but then they're laughing, and the woman facing me finally faces me and I lift my empty glass and she lifts hers.

"You shouldn't do that," I say.

"Why not?"

"It's bad luck to toast with an empty glass."

"I've never heard that before," she says.

"Maybe I made it up."

"If you made it up, it's not true."

"But it could be. Let's get these glasses filled just in case. The round's on us."

"Only if we drink to luck," the fat man says. "That's the only stipulation."

Two deep dimples frame his smile. I can see him charming his patients before he lays his fat hands on them.

Both women are facing me now, and the one who had her back turned holds my eyes long enough for me to know. The bartender puts a new round of drinks in front of us.

The first woman wears a turquoise bracelet and I tell her I saw that same color turquoise in New Mexico during a cross-country trip with a friend. The woman says she drove across Italy in a miniature Fiat and nearly plunged off the Amalfi Coast. The other woman says she drove a stick shift in Ireland, the roads too small for two cars. The fat man tells us about a desert Jeep ride, sliding down dunes, treacherous winds, sand blowing so hard it stung. They talk about best meals abroad, most adventurous foods tasted. Guinea pigs roasted on a spit in Peru. Fugu sashimi in Japan, the threat of a poisoned piece. The fat man describes a Bedouin camp he visited in the Sinai and the pleasure of eating lamb with his hands off large silver trays. He orders more drinks. He orders more oysters. The women are laughing and the fat man is laughing and time's starting to skip.

"Listen," I say to the two women. "Happy hour's about to end and none of us are taking any trips tonight. We're stuck in New York, so why don't we get some dinner? The

Strip House has great steaks and our new friend told me he'd like to take us out. I say we take him up on his offer."

"My offer stands, but only if we eat to luck," he says and they laugh. "That's the only stipulation."

The two women don't protest. There's me, so it won't look like they're dating a fat man, and they're enjoying the doctor's company. He's loose now, talking easy, funny, more than a fat man.

He signs off on his credit card, puts his hands on the bar and stands. He's even bigger standing up, his back two man-widths across. He breathes heavy, from the fat and the alcohol and maybe the expectation of a big steak dinner. He puts his hand on my shoulder, gives me a quick nod, and we walk outside, catch a cab.

They're laughing, drunk laughing, talking. Even the cab driver's laughing. The fat man's sitting in front, the back of his neck flushed. I could let them off, take the cab the rest of the way downtown, ring her buzzer, walk through her door. I could go to a bar, drink alone. I could find a wall to punch.

The Strip House is warm, red walls and red leather banquettes and the bar's crowded, the tables full, the waiters moving, everyone eating, talking, shouting, alcohol loud. I've been here with Paul. I've been here with Paul and Mel. Sometimes he just wanted a good steak after work. I'd put on the one suit I owned, like I'd also worked a full day downtown, and he'd tell me I washed up well. I can take being here, can take it with the alcohol. I can take being there if I have to. Showering with men. Shitting with men. Eating with men, rows and rows of men. I'll pretend I'm eating in the best steak house, meat salted and grilled perfectly, and I'll take it.

The doctor is larger than life, a celebrity of genetic proportions. The maître d' knows he'll bottleneck the bar and the women are pretty enough. I look at my knuckles. Folded skin too white and blood still wet. The maître d's taking us to a table in back and I'm walking through the prison mess hall and make my eyes hard.

The doctor waits for the three of us to slide into the red booth. He puts his hands on the table and lowers himself into a chair. We order cocktails. We order steaks. He orders two sides of goose fat potatoes. I go to the bathroom, wash my knuckles, look in the mirror, keep myself from saying his name, saying her name.

We eat. He orders dessert. My stomach's full of meat.

He's telling a story about a fellow doctor at his convention who admitted passing out at the sight of blood, who couldn't even order a rare steak for fear he'd go down and they're laughing. One of the women touches the fat man's arm. I picture him in a white robe, stethoscope around his neck, taking vitals with his fat hands and I look at my hand, look if it's steady, my hand holding my drink and I don't want to be here.

"What kind of doctor are you?" I say.

"A good luck doctor," he says and the women laugh.

"Really. What kind of doctor are you?"

"Has everyone digested their food?" he says. He's completely focused on the women. He's thinking he has a real shot and maybe he does. He could always get a hooker, but two free women for all night is a prize. I can see right through his eyes, right to his thoughts.

"What kind?" I say.

He turns to me, smiles, his eyes squinty and red.

"I'm a gastroenterologist," he says. "I'm a stomach doctor. Amply qualified, don't you think? I actually specialize in stomach staplings. I take fat people and make them less fat."

His smile goes away.

"Don't ask," he says. "It's the obvious question, but don't ask. With me, it's biological. It's in my thyroid, not my stomach. But when patients see me, they relax. It's all relative, right? I haven't met many men bigger than I am. They come to my office and I help them and now most of them lead normal lives. They have wives and children and by all reports they're happy."

"Tell me something," I say.

"Is it an obvious question?"

"It's a personal question. And since I won't ever see you again, I'll ask it."

The women are listening, I feel them listening, but they're background, like the waiters and busboys moving around, out there somewhere.

"If I went to prison. If I had to stop drinking just like that. What would happen? What would happen if I had to just sit there and think, hour after hour, day after day with-out a drink?"

"What are we talking about?"

"Okay. Just the drinking. I drink too much. What would happen if I had to stop drinking?"

"Physiologically?"

"You're the doctor."

He puts his fat hands flat on the table.

"They have programs in prison," he says.

"But what would happen?"

"It depends how much you drink."

"I can take it," I say.

"You're a wall puncher," he says. "You like to see how much you can take."

"Part of me isn't scared at all. Part of me doesn't care."

I look at my hands. Knuckles skinned. Fingers less swollen. I've slowed a little, slowed since I met her grieving for her sister, since we drank heavy that first night. But I could start again. Start heavy again. Drink heavy. Like I'm drinking now. Time-skip drinking. Like remembering. Re-member heavy instead of pretending everything's okay until it is.

"You'll take what you can take," he's saying. "But your body will take over. If you cut down before you go in, it will be easier. If you don't, it will be harder. But ultimately your body will take over and do what it must."

"Like jumping."

"I suppose. Like a lot of things. The brain starts things

off and it sends the impulse, but then the body takes over. After a while mind over matter really is just a saying that means nothing. The body wins no matter what anyone says."

I stand. There's a drink in front of me. I drink it down.

"He took you to dinner." I'm looking at the women. "He kept you entertained. He has a room at The Plaza. If you're fair, you'll go back with him. That's your sentence if you want to think of it that way."

The women don't say anything. But they're listening.

I'm looking at him. "Thanks for dinner. I'm full."

"Your body is full. So you stopped eating. That's a good start."

I'm forcing myself to walk straight. Through glowing Strip House red to sidewalk gray.

I'm forcing myself to walk straight. I'm looking down, like looking for money, like looking for the sparkle in the concrete, counting the squares, squares to get through.

I recognize her building.

I focus, remember, press.

Her voice. My voice.

Buzz.

Door.

Stairs.

Sandra. Standing by the door.

"Long time," she says.

"I know."

"You kind of disappeared."

"I know."

"You're drunk."

"I am."

"You smell like meat. When I was a kid, whenever our dog ate meat, my parents kicked him out of the house because he smelled. That's how you smell."

"What else do I smell like?"

"I don't know."

"I might be going to jail."

"What did you do?"

"Doing time. I know about time. I can make time skip forever."

I'm walking through the room. I'm walking to her bed.

"I can. I can drink and punch walls and keep it skipping forever."

I'm on her bed.

"I can," I say.

My legs are heavy. My eyes are heavy. My eyes are closed.

"I'm not that tough," I say.

"No one's that tough."

"But I'm not. I'm not that tough."

"Okay," she says.

"I'm not."

She's taking off my shoes.

I wake. I'm thirsty. She brings me water.

I wake. I hold the puke down in my throat.

I wake. I hear the shower, water hitting.

I wake.

"I'm going to work," she says.

"Thank you for taking me in."

"Don't make this a habit."

"I won't. I have to tell you something."

She sits on her bed. Her hands are relaxed, her fingers stained blue.

"I'm waiting," I say.

"Waiting for what?"

"My friend Paul had a wife. I'm waiting for her. I'm waiting for Paul's wife. She's the one I have to care for."

She's looking at me, steady, steady. Her eyes are something else than sad. I don't know all the ways her eyes go. Her eyes stay like that, stay there.

"Listen," she says. "I'm not ready either. We had a good few weeks. I know that's all it was."

"Thank you."

She moves her eyes. She stands up from her bed.

"Sleep it off," she says.

"Thank you," I say.

I run.

I stand.

I sleep.

I wait for Mel.

Her voice stops me.

I pick up the phone.

"I'm back," Mel says.

"You're in the city?"

"I am," she says.

"I'm back in New York," she says. "Meet me. Meet me at Angel's Share."

It's almost evening, but it's still light out, still clear.

"You've been drinking," I say.

"You can tell."

"I can tell."

"You're the expert. Yes. I've been out. I've been out and out and out. I've been non-stop out. I've been out so much Gibril wants me to stop, but he never stops me. He's not like you. He doesn't keep the pieces of his life separate. I was surprised at first. He can't even concentrate on his business dealings sometimes. Sometimes all he can do is care about me and I know he wants to stop, but he can't stop. I'm like a bad pet he loves so much he can't get rid of it. Not like you. You don't care that way. That can be very attractive. I bet all the girls who take you to Angel's Share think they can find that part of you they think is there."

"When did you get back?"

"I'm right, aren't I?"

"Sure. When did you get back?"

"You see? You see? I'm right."

I look across my room. Floor. Bed. Dresser. Wall. As anonymous as a hotel room.

"I got back this morning," she says. "Meet me at Angel's Share."

I hear the sound of ice against glass, of alcohol going down.

"Do you ever dream about him?" she says.

"I think about him."

"You don't dream?"

"I daydream about him. I think about things we did together."

"What things?"

"Before things. I try to think of before things."

I hear the ice, the sip.

"I understand why Gibril wanted me away from here. Even when he was saying it was for me, it was for himself first, and that's what people do. We're almost all guilty of that. I had to be away from here for me. I couldn't even face downtown."

I wait.

"I only see him when I'm awake. People think I drink to forget. I know that's what they think, but they're wrong. I drink to remember. It changes the way the day moves and I remember longer stretches of time and then I'm with him for longer than just looking at a photograph and seeing his face. And I keep thinking if I pass out, maybe he'll be in my dreams. And then I won't have to remember. He'll be there."

Her words stop her. I can hear her breathing.

"I haven't passed out like that yet," she says.

I count her breaths. One and. Two and. Three and. Like pouring a generous pour. It's light out and I'm tired.

"I heard when someone dead visits you in a dream and it's a good dream, then that person is okay, wherever he is. That hasn't happened yet. I think Paul would give me one of those if it were true."

"Maybe he will," I say.

"But you're not sure. I can hear it in your voice. I'm not that drunk. I'm never that drunk."

One and two and.

"New York City," she says.

Three and.

"Meet me there," she says.

I hear ice against glass and she hangs up the phone.

I get in the shower. I don't have to. I can show up as beat-up as she sounds. I'll be beat-up soon enough. I haven't dreamed of him, but I've dreamed of her. I've dreamed of being inside her, dreamed it when I'm half awake, half not, inside some woman, moving in and out, in and out, anatomically, automatically, and then I'm in Mel. I wash the soap off me, turn the water off.

I dress. I go down. It's almost warm, almost spring. But there's nothing new in the air, just the illusion that comes from buds on trees, the smell of growth, as if the soil is trying to fortify what's above, trying to reach through all the pavement and concrete, but only the scent makes it.

I walk. West Village. Washington Square. The buildings of NYU. The library is crowded. Grace Church a few blocks north. The spire's already lit and taller than anything around. Cooper Union. I cross Third Avenue.

Angel's Share.

I walk up the stairs, for her, for him, for me, I don't know, walk through the restaurant, open the door.

She's here. Her hair is cut short, which brings out her cheekbones, which makes her look more gaunt than I remember, trying to remember her before. There's a man next to her talking and he touches her arm and I know that touch, testing to see how far he can go now, how far he'll be able to go later. I could go. I could turn around and go. I ran from Paul.

I walk to Mel and stop just behind her and, as if she smells me, she turns and her eyes don't move, all the time in the world.

"David," she says and it's a different kind of skip, a heart skip, right there.

She kisses my cheek. She nods at the man she's been talking to and her eyes, so light, as close to white as blue can go, almost lifeless when she makes them that way, are enough. The man walks away. He'd do better anywhere but next to her.

Her eyes are on me.

"Back in Angel's Share," she says.

"Here we are."

"It was yours first, but you did bring me here."

"It's a free country."

Mel finishes her martini and looks at the glass.

"I've been drinking martinis these days," she says.

"No olives."

"No olives. Very dry."

"Just pass the bottle of vermouth over the glass and it's done."

"That easy," she says.

I order a bourbon on the rocks and a dry martini for Mel and watch the bartender pour. No mulled fruit. No mixers. Just alcohol.

"Li's not here tonight," Mel says.

"Maybe it's his night off."

The bartender puts down the drinks, nods.

"Welcome back," I say and touch Mel's glass.

"Thank you," she says and then smiles.

"What's so funny?"

"I remember how formal I was the first night you took me here. I said thank you at the subway station like we'd never met."

"It's a pleasure to meet you," I say.

"The pleasure's all mine," she says.

It's crowded in Angel's Share. It's always crowded in Angel's Share and the world always feels almost far away. Through the large windows, the view of the street looks like a movie set, as if the city were one big prop, and if it were, if it were just a set, if the falling buildings were just a movie, some high-tech, special-effects masterpiece, I would put down my drink and do my own dance on the streets, a singing-in-the-rain dance of joy, whether it were raining or not.

"So what's new in the city?" she says.

"Nothing's new."

"Yes there is."

"Tell me then. What's new?"

"They're almost done with the digging. I read about it in the papers over there. They're going to send family members official letters telling us they're officially done. And that will be that."

Mel takes a long swallow from her martini. "Has the weather been as good as they said in the papers?"

"It's been clear almost every day."

"I read they didn't miss one day of digging. It's like a miracle if you believe such things. It was beautiful out the day it happened and it's stayed beautiful the whole time since. Maybe the days will stay clear forever, just days and days and days of clear days."

"Maybe."

"We know better than that," she says and her almost-smile, empty and tired, brings the outside world that's not a set right into the bar.

"Did you eat?" I say.

"Let's drink our dinner tonight. Are you in shape for that?"

I make a muscle for her.

"I've seen you do the same thing for other women."

"It's one of the things I do."

"One night I saw you and Paul when you were out to-gether. We had just started seeing each other. He said you might be going to a certain bar and I was out with a friend and we ended up there. Man Ray. It was Man Ray. I watched you talking to a woman and you made a muscle."

"Did you purposely go there, or did you just end up there?"

"I purposely went there. But I knew Paul would be good."

"What did you know about me?"

"I didn't know you."

The bartenders are working hard. One cocktail seems more complex than the next. Bottles are tipped. Shakers are shaken. Drinks are placed on beverage napkins. The bartenders nod their heads.

"In France, there were American flags everywhere when I got there," Mel says. "But before I left I didn't notice so many of them."

"You should have told The Arab to buy more flags. I bet he would have lined the streets of Paris with American flags if you'd told him to."

"We only went to Paris once."

"All you had to do was say the word."

"All I had to do," she says and drinks.

"When did he fall in love with you?"

"It doesn't matter."

"When?"

"It took some time."

She's looking at her martini glass, the thin stem, the graceful V holding gin.

"One afternoon we were sitting on the beach at Villefranche. It was just like the postcard. The semi-circle of beach with the old town behind going up the mountain and that day the sun was so high above the water it looked too far away to be the sun. He liked to watch me swim and that afternoon I swam far out. The water was very cold, but I wanted to keep swimming. I wanted to swim to the place in the water that was directly under the sun. I knew that was impossible. When I turned around to swim back, I saw him far away. He was standing on the beach, waving his arms, and he was calling for me. I hadn't even heard him I was so far out. When I got back to the beach he put a towel around me like I was sick, like I was sick from exertion, and his face was worried. I felt it in his touch. He loved me so much he was scared to lose me."

"That was the moment."

"That's when I knew," she says.

"You didn't know before?"

"I don't know."

"You didn't know he would fall for you?"

"I was thinking about me."

She tilts her martini glass, just a little, and the gin moves, settles.

"I don't know," she says. "You don't believe me. I don't know if I believe me. I don't know."

"You went there. You'll live with it."

"I thought we weren't living."

"I thought we were pretending we were."

"You're right," she says. "We were."

"When they're done digging, it's over," she says. "It's like a burial, only opposite. When they take out that last shovel full of debris, it's over. Dead and buried. Or dead and not buried."

She lifts the martini to her mouth, drinks, puts the glass down.

"I'm stopping tonight," she says.

"Stopping?"

"Tonight's my last night out. I wanted to spend it with you."

"What happens after tonight?"

"I'm going back to work. I'm going to rely on myself. I'm going to try to live again, but not pretend-living. I want to live like some of what I was with Paul. Some of what I was before it happened and before I regressed and became the stupid kind of young."

She finishes her martini and puts her hands on the bar. Her wedding ring is gold like the best bourbons and scotches displayed along the bar's top shelf, the mirror behind doubling every bottle.

"Was that your last drink?" I say.

"No. I'll order another soon. And maybe another after that. And then I'll stop."

"A four-course dinner."

"Or a five-course dinner. It's my last dinner. I want to

make it memorable."

"If you drink enough it won't be memorable anymore. You'll forget almost everything."

"I won't forget almost everything. I won't let myself drink that much."

"I will."

"Don't. Not tonight. I don't want you to drink so much you'll forget everything."

"I can't forget everything."

I order two more drinks.

"We're the easiest customers in the bar. A simple martini. A simple bourbon."

"Two easy customers in Angel's Share," Mel says.

We watch the bartender. His hands move expertly. He fills the martini glass with a flourish, then places the drinks in front of us, one nod per drink.

"To your last night out," I say.

"Cheers," she says and we touch glasses.

"Are you so sure you can stop?

"Can't you stop?"

"I don't care if I can stop or not."

We watch the bartenders work. We listen to the conversations around us. We listen to the laughter. Everyone seems to be having a good time.

Mel's new cell phone rings. She looks at the number and doesn't answer. Her cell phone rings again.

"Excuse me," she says.

I can't hear his words, but I know it's him. It's too loud

in here, but I know he's talking, trying. She holds the phone to her ear, waiting for him to finish. The only word she keeps saying is No. She says No each time without malice, without expression. He's still talking. She says No again and waits and then she says Angel's Share. She closes the phone and puts it away.

"He wouldn't get off. He wouldn't get off until I told him where I was."

She repeats herself when she's drunk.

We drink and wait.

After the towers fell, thousands of people stood along the West Side Highway to watch the tragic parade. Fire trucks and ambulances and police cars from all over the country. Buses full of rescue workers and supplies. Garbage trucks and pickup trucks and eighteen-wheelers with empty cargo space to help with the digging. All going downtown. The vehicles passed and the people applauded and I applauded too. I'm not sure why. I think it was because we were all Americans, forced to remember we were Americans, and we were coming together, working together. To help. To hope. And then I saw the fighter jet circling Manhattan, so high up it was a speck of glitter in the sky, and the anger shot through my balls and all I wanted was for that jet to fly over the ocean and over the desert and finish the ones who'd finished my friend.

The Arab is walking through the bar, handsome in his perfectly-cut suit, his eyes already on Mel. Mel stays looking at her drink. His eyes are still striking, flecks of blue in the brown, but up close he looks exhausted. He shakes my hand, his grip without strength, and he keeps his hand in my hand as if he doesn't know what else to do. I let go and he puts his hand on the back of Mel's chair, not touching her back, not touching her hair, and he looks at her looking at her drink.

"You can't," he says.

"We've gone over this."

"That's not good enough."

"Good or bad," she says. "I won't see you anymore."

"Let's take a walk."

"I don't want to take a walk."

"Please. I'd rather have this conversation in private."

"David knows me."

"He doesn't know us."

"He knows Paul."

The Arab's pupils narrow. Mel's looking at her martini glass, but maybe she's blurring her eyes, forcing them to stay so unfocused there are no lines, only shapes blending into each other.

"What did I do?" he says.

His voice is quiet, not a whisper but at the place just before a note breaks.

"Tell me," he says. "Please."

"I don't want you here," she says.

"I didn't forget your husband. You can't blame me for that."

Mel's mouth is closed. There's no space between her

lips.

"I understand you're still grieving," he says. "I understand you need more time. Of course, I understand. I'm prepared to wait for you and I want to wait for you."

"What do you understand?"

"I understand something terrible happened."

"Did you ever lose your spouse, Gibril?"

"No."

She drinks the rest of her martini. The bartender comes over, looks at the three of us, moves away.

"Every night," she says. "Every night I was with you I was with Paul. Every night I thought of my husband. I was never really with you."

"You can't say that."

"You got me away from here when I needed not to face downtown. That was very generous of you and I've thanked you many times. But I was never with you, Gibril."

"You were with me," he says. "I heard you."

"You heard me?"

"You were with me when you were with me."

"You don't know where I was."

I'm standing next to him, but I'm watching too, watching me standing next to him, and I'm watching her.

He puts his hand around her arm

"Mel," he says. "Look at me."

Mel looks at him, but not like he's the only one around. She's looking at him out of habit, a blind person turning to the direction of a voice and pretending to see.

"Don't go away like that," he says.

Mel looks at him.

"Don't do that."

She looks at him.

"Mel."

Her eyes don't change.

"I love you," he says.

One and two and.

He smashes his hand against the bar.

Angel's Share stops. The music is there, music that's always there in the background, but now it's the only sound. Even the bartenders have stopped moving.

I'm standing. Balanced. Ready. My hands fists. But his hand stays flat against the bar. He's watching Mel and he sees what I see. Her eyes haven't moved.

He removes his hand from the bar and, like the way he shook my hand, not sure how long to keep it there, his hand stays suspended between the bar and his body, unnaturally, like he doesn't know what to do with it. He looks at his hand. He lowers his hand to his side. He walks out of Angel's Share.

I look around. Some of the drinkers are still looking at where he left. Some of them are looking at Mel. Then they turn back to their friends, back to what they were talking about, and to their drinks.

"You broke him," I say. "I didn't think I'd care, but I actually feel sorry for that man."

"I didn't set out to break anyone."

"Then you're absolved."

"Obviously not."

I have enough alcohol in me. I can say what I want. Maybe I'll remember. Maybe I won't. I can be as careless as Mel.

"Did you ever do that to Paul? Something like that?"

"Never."

"Did you ever go that far away?"

"What are you asking?"

"I can understand The Arab needing to hit something."

"I'm sure. You're the one who punches walls."

"I don't really know what you were like with Paul. I thought I did, but after you went to France I thought I might be completely wrong. You left. You left with another man. Like that."

Mel picks up my glass from the bar and looks at the bourbon and ice.

"Husband," she says. "When I first got married the word sounded so strange when I said it out loud. It didn't sound natural. Then one day it did."

She finishes my drink and puts down the glass.

"I left with another man like that. And you stayed in New York. And you slept downtown. And you kept vigil over his body that's not even a body anymore. But he was my husband. Don't pretend you were more." Her eyes are on my eyes, like I'm the only one in the world, like a lie. "And don't pretend you didn't leave. You didn't see Paul for a long time. You didn't talk to Paul and you didn't see him.

You didn't leave New York, but you left him. You left him.
That's all. And then he was dead. And I won't pretend to
know what you're feeling."

Mel moves her eyes.

My breaths steady.

My body relaxes.

Like after a long run. You finally stop and your breathing slows and your body's loose from all those miles and
then, a few minutes later, you hardly remember how hard
it was.

"I promised him," I say. "It was after, but it was a promise. I promised him I'd wait for you to fall. Even when I was
drunk, even when I was blacked out, even when you were
gone, I was waiting."

I want time to skip, want to be in the between part, the
blacked-out part, the nothing, but it's not skipping.

"I waited for you."

"I know," she says.

"No. I waited for you. I was waiting for you apart from
him and I hated myself for that. I promised Paul I'd wait,
but it wasn't a pure promise. It was a promise I made for
you."

Mel takes my hand. She opens my fist.

"You shouldn't hate yourself for that," she says.

"He wouldn't hate you for that," she says.

She takes her hands from my hand and puts her hands
in her lap like a prayer.

I haven't been here since Paul was killed. It looks the same, as if Paul could be standing in the living room ready to greet me. If only Paul were here. If only he were standing in front of me in this living room, right now. I'd have it out with him. I'd ask him why he said the things he said even if I know. I'd ask him so I could answer him and not run. I'd tell him he was wrong about me, that I was going to try to start living, that I wasn't just a little man. And Paul would smile the way he often smiled when he was with me. Like he was up to something. Like there was a joke in what we'd said. And more. Like he cared, openly, warmly, happy to be with me. If I can make peace with Paul, if I can start living, open-eyed living, without look-at-me poses, without Hollywood cluttering my movement, maybe I'll be able to smile like that.

I'm here.

Paul's not here.

Mel is here.

She sits on the couch. I stay standing.

"Sit with me," she says.

I walk across the room and sit next to her, not touching. I look out the window that looks south. There are no shades on the window, no curtains or blinds, and I wonder if she lets herself look out. She leans back into the couch and crosses her legs.

"I've lived your life for a while," she says. "Even in

France I never slept in. I left the bedroom and took long walks in the morning. They were abrupt, early mornings and I thought of you every time I walked. Paul told me you never brought them home to your place, so you could walk when you were ready to walk, and every morning I pictured you leaving their apartments. I pictured you walking out the door and going down and drinking a Yoo-hoo on the way home."

"You know all my tricks."

"It's funny how something sticks in your head and stays there. It becomes part of the pattern. Thinking of your pattern became part of my pattern, so I pictured you every time. Do you really see right through? When you're done, at the moment you're done, do you really see right through the world at that moment?"

"He told you everything, didn't he?"

"Yes," she says.

"I used to think I saw right through."

"And now?"

"Now I don't know."

She puts her hand around the back of my neck, the move I've used so many times, and takes my head to hers, my mouth to hers.

We kiss until we stop.

It's so quiet ghosts could appear. But they don't. Maybe we're too far uptown. It's just the after-kiss in this room.

I know her eyes. I know her mouth. I know her body. But she's out of character from the Mel I knew. Like a wedge of glass has been pushed into her, refracting what is whole into parts, a Picasso painting of a woman. Her drinking, her leaving New York, her morning walks, are pronounced pieces. It's not all of her. But part of her. It's her last night out. She says it's her last night out. She wants to extract the glass and make herself whole again.

I try to see Mel like before, but I can't. Before. After. I look at her a long time.

"I already knew how you'd kiss," she says. "You knew how I'd kiss too."

"No surprises."

"None."

"He wouldn't have done that."

"I like to think he would have gone a little crazy without me. Or without you."

She takes my hand.

"Tell me something about him I don't know," she says.

"You know everything I know and more. I can't tell you anything."

"There must be something. One thing."

I could tell her about Tijuana, about fucking twenty-dollar whores in five-dollar motel rooms, but that would cut into Paul, make him Picasso-like in her head, and when the North Tower fell that created enough fragments. I think of him. I think of heat. I think of collapse. I can't separate the day.

"We were walking," I say. "We were going to get a burger and a beer at the Corner Bistro the way we did so many times and on the way we passed a fortune teller. She had set up a table on the street and Paul sat down. He'd never been to a fortune teller and neither had I. He gave her his palm and she looked at it closely, like there was meaning in every line. After a full minute she looked up. She told him he would be successful. She told him he would be happy. And the last thing she told him was that he'd already met the woman he'd spend the rest of his life with. Paul looked at me and he looked at the fortune teller and he asked her when exactly he'd met this woman he'd be with for the rest of his life. She studied his palm for a moment and smiled. She told him he'd met her within the last three days. It had been three days since he'd met you. Paul couldn't believe it. He asked where in his palm she saw that, what line in his palm, so he could show the line to you. She told him it wasn't in his palm at all. She said she saw it in his smile and she saw it most in his eyes. Before we left, the fortune teller told us never to tell anyone how the secret to palm reading wasn't in the palm. I don't know if he ever told you that story. I'm guessing he didn't."

"The rest of his life with me," Mel says.

"That's a nice story," she says.

Mel stands and leaves the room. I listen for a door to close.

I look out the window. It's dark out, but the window cuts the dark, cuts the distance out there.

"I thought of Paul every time."

She's standing naked. I recognize her body.

"I thought of him every time," she says. "I kept my eyes closed and thought of him. I need to see if I can keep my eyes open."

She goes into the bathroom and turns on the light and waits.

I stand. I walk, aware of each step, look-at-me aware, like walking a runway, like the first time I walked, a Soho store showing off its fall line. I walked across the elevated platform and kept my eyes distant the way you're supposed to when clothes are hung on a body, eyes looking ahead, lit but untouchable, seeing nobody. I was walking and watching myself walk, watching my body, watching my distance and it was easy. Her pale eyes too pale. My dead eyes too dead. I've seen my eyes in bathroom mirrors. I'm walking, runway walking, across her living room, but it's not easy and I'm at the end of the runway and I stop.

"David," she says.

She turns on the shower and gets in. I take off my clothes and get in. The water is warm.

She washes my neck, my back, my arms, my chest, my stomach, my cock, my legs, my feet. She washes herself. She turns off the water and gets out and I get out.

She dries me. She dries herself.

She walks to the bedroom.

She gets on the bed.

I get on the bed.

I take her head in my hand and kiss her. She kisses back. Soft. Hard. She takes my head and lifts it hard.

"I want you to look at me," she says. "And I want to look at you."

She opens her legs and I put my cock into her.

I fuck her. I make her rhythm my rhythm, make my rhythm her rhythm. She holds tight, hands tight against my arms, legs tight against my back, eyes open on my eyes and I keep my eyes on hers. Her eyes are almost white. I watch her eyes and move. I watch her mouth and move. Her mouth is open and her eyes are open.

And she screams. One long scream that doesn't stop, that sounds like it will never stop, a scream about everything, everything, everything falling out of her.

And I fuck her.

And she screams.

And I fuck her.

And her scream slows.

And I fuck her.

And her legs relax and her arms and her hands and her scream stops.

And I stop.

Her eyes are still open.

Her eyes are open and she starts to cry. She cries, almost silent, the longest exhales, like a sound should come out, but there's almost no sound. The long exhales become shorter. The almost-silent becomes silent. I watch her all the way down.

I'm here.

I'm sitting on my bed. I've run. I've stood. I've been sitting on my bed for a while. It's a new part of my daily ritual. I'm tired of not moving, but I'm too tired to move.

I haven't seen Mel for weeks. I haven't spoken to Mel for weeks.

I spend my days running and then standing and then sitting on my bed. I don't drink. And so time isn't skipping.

In the morning the light woke us. She got up and I heard her moving and I heard the bathroom door close. She didn't come back to bed.

My clothes were folded neatly on the couch. I dressed and left.

I sit. I think about Mel. I think about Paul. I look at my hands and they're not fists.

From here I can see the East River, the buildings in Queens, the line-up of jets coming into LaGuardia, moving so slowly you'd think they'd drop, but they don't. They move forward, lower and lower and then I can't see them anymore, but I'm sure they've landed safely. The roof is in the Bronx. The building's a five-story walk-up with a car repair business on the ground floor and apartments above. When we got here, a man in work coveralls, retro *Esso* stitched on his chest pocket, walked us around the garage, showed us the leaks, walked us up the stairs to the top floor, knocked on each door before he opened it, pointed to the water damage staining each ceiling.

I take off my work gloves and wipe my hand across my forehead. It's early. I'm sweating. Tar stains my forearms. I watch another plane come in.

Kazanoff is on the other side of the roof, his knees bent, also spreading tar. He doesn't look like a laborer. He doesn't look like the owner of a roof repair business. He has a kind face, kind eyes. The lines of his bifocals cut his irises in two and his hands, even with tar under his fingernails and flashing streaking his skin, are fine and thin. He looks frail, but his forearms have ridges of muscle and he works hard and steady.

There's Kazanoff. There's a Mexican worker named Jesse, strong and square-shouldered. There's me. Kazanoff has other jobs going around the city, other workers working other roofs, but he's here with us. It's the first day on this job and he likes to be around for first days.

It's my sixth roof. The first job took five days with four men working, a warehouse roof in the Bronx pockmarked with holes, bubbles in the tar, and torn tarpaper that we had to strip before we spread fresh tar and silver flashing. I was sore after the first day, in my back and shoulders and thighs and wrists. I was more sore the second day. I was less sore the third day. The next job was a four-story residential brownstone in East Harlem. The other jobs blended into each other, hole after hole, sweeping debris each morning, spreading tar over small holes, torching strips of tar paper over bigger holes, outlining edges with aluminum, a patchwork of black and silver. On the worst holes, Kazanoff uses wire mesh and tar paper and tar, filling them in, smoothing them over. I sleep well at night. I'm up early. My face is tan. My hands are callused. I stand at the Art Students League on the weekend. I told them I was cast in a film that shoots weekdays, a shoot that will last only a few weeks, just in case. There's no camera here. Just me. Kazanoff. Jesse. The roof. The drums of tar. The tin of aluminum. The brushes. The trowels. The industrial push-broom, thick-bristled. I'm five stories closer to the sun.

I put my work gloves back on. I start spreading tar, like frosting a cake, smooth strokes of black. My muscles relax into the work. I move from hole to hole, filling, smoothing. The time moves.

We break for lunch.

We go down to the neighborhood deli. That's the routine. At the job by eight. Lunch at twelve. This place has hot sandwiches and the three of us order chicken parmigiana heroes. Jesse gets a pack of cupcakes for dessert. We take the food back to the roof and eat. A dog barks, a big-sounding bark, maybe smelling food, then gets bored and stops. A plane banks, straightens, rising at a gentle angle. We don't talk, but it's not like we're eating alone. We don't talk when we work. We work silently together, listening to the city's sounds and the closer sounds of roof repair.

Another plane banks and rises. Kazanoff finishes his

water and wipes the back of his forearm across his mouth.
I hold the trash bag open and Jesse shoots his balled-up
sandwich wrapper, scores. He looks at the sun and stretches. I think Paul would like this work. We wouldn't have to
talk either.

Kazanoff lights up the torch and burns tar paper into
the roof, working methodically, his face never changing
even when the flame sputters. Jesse and I paint the outside
edges with aluminum coating. My arms are streaked black
and silver. There are scratch lines on my arm. I don't know
how I get them, but they're there every day.

The time moves. My muscles feel long and relaxed and
I never lose my breath. The alcohol in my blood was taking my breath away. I ran and drank and the drinking took
away the running and the next morning a flight of stairs
would wind me.

Kazanoff finishes the last square and Jesse starts outlining the square with aluminum coating. I pick up the broom.
Kazanoff showed me how to use my arms and not my back.
We sweep to start the job. We sweep to end the job. I gather dirt, paper, glass, shreds of tarpaper, three bottle caps,
sweep the piles onto a flat of cardboard, throw it all away.

We undress on the roof. I remove my tar-stained sweat-
shirt, my tar-stained T-shirt, my tar-stained jeans. I put
them in a new trash bag for tomorrow. I'm in underwear
and socks, almost naked, and no one is drawing.

We put on our clean clothes and go down. The truck
is parked at the corner. We throw the broom and brushes

onto the truck bed, put in the cans of tar and aluminum, put in the trash bags with our stained clothes. It's light out, still hours until evening. The seats are warm from the sun. Kazanoff drives.

I'm meeting Mel.

Not in Angel's Share. Not in any bar. We're meeting at Central Park on the corner of Columbus Circle and I'm sitting on the steps below the fountain, dry in winter, still dry now. Some pigeons walk along the steps pecking at discarded food. Along 59th Street the horses and carriages are lined up. Some of the horses tap their hooves against the street. Some bury their heads in their water buckets, tails moving left and right.

A messenger sets down his bike and sits on the steps near me. He takes off his helmet and wipes the sweat from his face with his palms. He takes a sandwich from a paper bag and eats. His body looks relaxed, the kind of relaxed that comes from working hard. I can almost taste his sandwich, how delicious it is after pedaling all those miles. When Garrett called to tell me charges had been dropped, I breathed. He said the Arab at the newsstand didn't want to testify against me. A pigeon approaches the messenger, pecks a crumb at his feet. The messenger stands and stretches his arms, then gets on his bike and rides off.

Seeing Mel stops me. I see me inside her. I almost hear

her scream. She's walking uptown, her back to downtown, her posture perfect. I stand and walk off the fountain steps and when she's in front of me I see the change. Her face is not so gaunt. Her eyes are not so pale.

"You look good," I say.

"Thank you."

"You're not living my life anymore."

"I don't know if I'm living my life," she says. "But you're right. I'm not living yours. You look good too. I can't remember the last time I saw you in daylight."

"You never did," I say and she laughs and I remember her laugh, her laugh from before, not too open-mouthed, not too loud. Her mouth looks like before too, more full, with only that space between her lips hinting at something darker.

"I haven't been here in a while," she says and her eyes move to the park and then back to me.

"Paul and I once challenged a thunderstorm right over there. We took off our shirts and faced the lightning. It was his idea. He wanted to feel alive."

Mel moves her eyes.

"Let's walk," she says.

Central Park is so busy it looks like summer vacation. Afternoon runners and bikers and people sitting on benches taking in the day and on the softball fields men are playing. The trees are nearly full. We get on the horse path and walk on the packed dirt that meanders through the trees.

"Smell that," she says. "The air's almost clean here."

"Almost."

"When I was a girl I spent all my free time outside. Now the outdoors feels like a luxury."

"When I was a boy I couldn't wait to grow up so I could move here."

"Here or anywhere?"

"I would have moved anywhere as long as it was away. But I wanted to move here. I wanted to live in Manhattan where all the action was."

"I don't know why I chose New York. When I was finishing college, I applied for jobs all over the country. Paul used to say he pulled me here."

Mel looks straight ahead like she always does when she walks. She's wearing a thin jacket and her hands are in her pockets. A park ranger on horseback comes down the path. The horse is thick, thick muscles and mane. The ranger keeps his eyes above us, scanning the woods, as if danger might be waiting around the bend, which it isn't. There aren't enough people in this part of the park and there's nothing to damage but trees.

"They call this the bridle path, don't they?" Mel says. "Horses and runners."

The horse and ranger pass, the horse's thick tail moving back and forth.

"I'm leaving New York," she says.

I stop walking and she stops. Her eyes go from looking straight ahead to looking straight at me.

"I wanted to see you before I left. I'm moving to Los

Angeles. We have an office there, and when I put in for a transfer they couldn't say no. I'm leaving tomorrow."

"Tomorrow."

"I know it's fast."

"Have you been to LA?"

"A few times," she says. "For work."

"I was there with Paul."

"I saw the photograph. The two of you in front of the Hollywood sign."

"It's not like here."

"Here's not like here to me," Mel says.

Her eyes are blue again, blue and clear. I could go west with her. I could leave New York in a day. I could fit everything I own in a few boxes and be ready.

"In a way he made it easy for me to leave," she says. "He's missing, so I can miss him anywhere."

We start walking again. Mel looking straight ahead. Me looking straight ahead. The sky is blue between the trees. The air is almost fresh.

We get to the reservoir. People are running around the loop, dirt easier on their feet than pavement. The wall that divides the reservoir, just above water level, looks like a runway for walking.

"Hollywood."

"What about Hollywood?" she says.

"He was right. One picture is enough."

We turn and walk back along the horse path. The sound of our feet on dirt. The sound of our feet on pavement. The tallest buildings in view. We walk out of the park and the city is before us. The traffic moves around Columbus Circle. Mel stops and for the first time in a long time her back isn't to downtown. She's looking south, in the direction of the hole.

"I'm starting to remember him beyond that day," she says. "Sometimes when I think of Paul I don't think about the building falling. Maybe I'll dream of him soon."

Mel is looking downtown. I'm looking downtown. I look up at the statue of Columbus standing on top of his pillar and like so many things in New York I notice him for the first time. He's looking downtown too.

"Did the lightning hit close?"

"Very close."

"Very close," she says. "And then it passed."

"I felt alive that day."

"You are alive. And I'm alive too."

Her eyes are blue and beautiful. I move my finger to her eyes and she closes them for me. I move my finger to her eyelid, closer, closer, but I don't touch it.

"That's when I knew. When he touched you there."

"Paul," she says.

"Paul," I say.

One and two and.

I move my finger away.

She opens her eyes.

"I'm going to say good bye. Walk me to the station."

People are coming out of their offices. The streets are

filling up. Rush hour has begun.

We cross the avenue. The green globe is lit. The station is open.

Mel doesn't say thank you. She doesn't laugh at the formality of it all. She kisses me on the cheek and then she walks down the stairs, perfect posture, looking straight ahead.

She is there.

She is gone.

Like that.

I wish to thank the following: Nava Renek and Tod Thilleman at Spuyten Duyvil for their time and effort, and for running a strong small press. Cecile Corona, Robert Lescher, Gena Hamshaw, Zahra El-Mekkawy and Rochana Rapkins—yours were the careful eyes that helped me see. Jeffrey Heiman, my great friend and colleague, the one I turn to when I need to turn a sentence around. Frida Lee for her smile and her warmth and so much more. To my mother and father and brother, always there—you already know my thanks. And to my students and colleagues at John Jay College of Criminal Justice where I teach writing, thank you for your support. The number we lost at John Jay College was sixty-eight.

ADAM BERLIN is the author of *Both Members of the Club* (Texas Review Press/winner of the 2012 Clay Reynolds Novella Prize), *Belmondo Style* (St. Martin's Press/winner of the Publishing Triangle's Ferro-Grumley Award) and *Headlock* (Algonquin Books of Chapel Hill). His stories and poetry have appeared in numerous journals. He teaches writing at CUNY's John Jay College of Criminal Justice in New York City and co-edits *J Journal: New Writing on Justice.* For more visit www.adamberlin.com

CEPHALONICAL SKETCHES   t thilleman

CLEF   j/j hastain & t thilleman

CLEOPATRA HAUNTS THE HUDSON   Sarah White

CLOUD FIRE   Katherine Hastings

COLUMNS: TRACK 2   Norman Finkelstein

COLLECTED POEMS OF LEV LOSEFF   (ed.) Henry Pickford

CONSCIOUSNESS SUITE   David Landrey

*THE CONVICTION & SUBSEQUENT
            LIFE OF SAVIOR NECK*   Christian TeBordo

CONVICTION'S NET OF BRANCHES   Michael Heller

THE CORYBANTES   Tod Thilleman

CROSSING BORDERS   Kowit & Silverberg

DAY BOOK OF A VIRTUAL POET   Robert Creeley

DAYLIGHT TO DIRTY WORK   Tod Thilleman

THE DESIRE NOTEBOOKS   John High

DETECTIVE SENTENCES   Barbara Henning

DIARY OF A CLONE   Saviana Stanescu

DIFFIDENCE   Jean Harris

DONNA CAMERON   Donna Cameron

DON'T KILL ANYONE, I LOVE YOU   Gojmir Polajnar

DRAY-KHMARA AS A POET   Oxana Asher

EGGHEAD TO UNDERHOOF   Tod Thilleman

ELSA   Tsipi Keller

EROTICIZING THE NATION   Leverett T. Smith, Jr.

THE EVIL QUEEN   Benjamin Perez

EXILED FROM THE WOMB   Adrian Sangeorzan

EXTREME POSITIONS   Stephen Bett

THE FARCE   Carmen Firan

FISSION AMONG THE FANATICS   Tom Bradley

THE FLAME CHARTS   Paul Oppenheimer

FLYING IN WATER   Barbara Tomash

FORM   Martin Nakell

FOUR SEASONS   Michael Forstrom

GESTURE THROUGH TIME   Elizabeth Block

GHOSTS!   Martine Bellen

GIRAFFES IN HIDING   Carol Novack

GNOSTIC FREQUENCIES   Patrick Pritchett

GOD'S WHISPER   Dennis Barone

GOWANUS CANAL, HANS KNUDSEN   Tod Thilleman

HALF-GIRL   Stephanie Dickinson

HE KNOWS WHAT A STICK IS   Russell Brickey

HIDDEN DEATH, HIDDEN ESCAPE   Liviu Georgescu

HOUNDSTOOTH   David Wirthlin

IDENTITY   Basil King

IN TIMES OF DANGER   Paul Oppenheimer

INCRETION   Brian Strang

INFERNO   Carmen Firan

INFINITY SUBSECTIONS   Mark DuCharme

INSOUCIANCE   Thomas Phillips

IN THAILAND WITH THE APOSTLES   Joanna Sit

INVERTED CURVATURES   Francis Raven

THE IVORY HOUR   Laynie Browne

JACKPOT   Tsipi Keller

THE JAZZER & THE LOITERING LADY   Gordon Osing

KISSING NESTS   Werner Lutz, trans. by Marc Vincenz

KNOWLEDGE   Michael Heller

LADY V.   D.R. Popa

LAST SUPPER OF THE SENSES   Dean Kostos

LAWFULLY WEDDED WIVES   Nona Caspers & Joell Hallowell

A LESSER DAY   Andrea Scrima

LET'S TALK ABOUT DEATH   M. Maurice Abitbol

LIBRETTO FOR THE EXHAUSTED WORLD   Michael Fisher

LIGHT HOUSE   Brian Lucas

*LIGHT YEARS: MULTIMEDIA IN THE
EAST VILLAGE, 1960-1966*   (ed.) Carol Bergé

LITTLE BOOK OF DAYS   Nona Caspers

LITTLE TALES OF FAMILY & WAR   Martha King

LONG FALL: ESSAYS AND TEXTS   Andrey Gritsman

LUNACIES   Ruxandra Cesereanu

LUST SERIES   Stephanie Dickinson

LYRICAL INTERFERENCE   Norman Finkelstein

MAINE BOOK   Joe Cardarelli (ed.) Anselm Hollo

MANNHATTEN   Sarah Rosenthal

MATING IN CAPTIVITY   Nava Renek

MEANWHILE   Gordon Osing

MEDIEVAL OHIO   Richard Blevins

MEMORY'S WAKE   Derek Owens

MERMAID'S PURSE   Laynie Browne

MIMING MINK   j/j hastain

MOBILITY LOUNGE   David Lincoln

MODERN ADVENTURES   Bill Evans

THE MOSCOVIAD   Yuri Andrukhovych

MULTIFESTO: A HENRI D'MESCAN READER (REMIX EDITION)   Davis Schneiderman

MY LAST CENTURY   Joanna Sit

THE NEW BEAUTIFUL TENDONS   Jeffery Beam

NIGHTHAWKS   Katherine Hastings

NIGHTSHIFT / AN AREA OF SHADOWS   Erika Burkart & Ernst Halter

NO PERFECT WORDS   Nava Renek

NO WRONG NOTES   Norman Weinstein

NORTH & SOUTH   Martha King

NOTES OF A NUDE MODEL   Harriet Sohmers Zwerling

THE NUMBER OF MISSING   Adam Berlin

OF ALL THE CORNERS TO FORGET   Gian Lombardo

ONE FOOT OUT THE DOOR   Lewis Warsh

ONÖNYXA & THERSEYN   T Thilleman

THE OPENING DAY   Richard Blevins

OUR FATHER   M.G. Stephens

OVER THE LIFELINE   Adrian Sangeorzan

PAGAN DAYS   Michael Rumaker

PART OF THE DESIGN   Laura E. Wright

PIECES FOR SMALL ORCHESTRA & OTHER FICTIONS   Norman Lock

A PLACE IN THE SUN   Lewis Warsh

THE POET : PENCIL PORTRAITS   Basil King

POLITICAL ECOSYSTEMS   J.P. Harpignies

POWERS: TRACK 3   Norman Finkelstein

THE PRISON NOTEBOOKS OF ALAN KRIEGER (TERRORIST)   Marc Estrin

THE PROPAGANDA FACTORY   Marc Vincenz

COLUMNS: TRACK 2   Norman Finkelstein

REMAINS TO BE SEEN   Halvard Johnson

RETELLING   Tsipi Keller

RIVERING   Dean Kostos

ROOT-CELLAR TO RIVERINE   Tod Thilleman

THE ROOTS OF HUMAN SEXUALITY   M. Maurice Abitbol

SAIGON AND OTHER POEMS   Jack Walters

A SARDINE ON VACATION   Robert Castle

SAVOIR FEAR   Charles Borkhuis

SECRET OF WHITE   Barbara Tomash

SEDUCTION   Lynda Schor

SEE WHAT YOU THINK   David Rosenberg

SEMI-SLEEP   Kenneth Baron

SETTLEMENT   Martin Nakell

SEX AND THE SENIOR CITY   M. Maurice Abitbol

SEXUAL HARASSMENT RULES   Lynda Schor

SKETCHES IN NORSE & FORRA   t thilleman

SKETCHES TZITZIMIME   t thilleman

SLAUGHTERING THE BUDDHA   Gordon Osing

THE SNAIL'S SONG   Alta Ifland

SOS: SONG OF SONGS OF SOLOMON   j/j hastain

THE SPARK SINGER   Jade Sylvan

SPIRITLAND   Nava Renek

STATE OF THE UNION   Susan Lewis

STRANGE EVOLUTIONARY FLOWERS   Lizbeth Rymland

SUDDENLY TODAY WE CAN DREAM   Rutha Rosen

THE SUDDEN DEATH OF...   Serge Gavronsky

THE TAKEAWAY BIN   Toni Mirosevich

THE TATTERED LION   Juana Culhane

TAUTOLOGICAL EYE   Martin Nakell

TED'S FAVORITE SKIRT   Lewis Warsh

THEATERS OF SKIN   Gordon Osing & Tom Carlson

THINGS THAT NEVER HAPPENED   Gordon Osing

THREAD   Vasyl Makhno

THREE MOUTHS   Tod Thilleman

THREE SEA MONSTERS   Tod Thilleman

THE TOMMY PLANS   Cooper Renner

TRACK   Norman Finkelstein

TRANSITORY   Jane Augustine

TRANSPARENCIES LIFTED FROM NOON   Chris Glomski

TRIPLE CROWN SONNETS   Jeffrey Cyphers Wright

TSIM-TSUM   Marc Estrin

TWELVE CIRCLES   Yuri Andrukhovych

VIENNA ØØ   Eugene K. Garber

UNCENSORED SONGS FOR SAM ABRAMS   (ed.) John Roche

UP FISH CREEK ROAD   David Matlin

VENICE IS FOR CATS   Nava Renek & Ethel Renek

WARP SPASM   Basil King

WATCHFULNESS   Peter O'Leary

WATCH THE DOORS AS THEY CLOSE   Karen Lillis

WALKING AFTER MIDNIGHT   Bill Kushner

WEST OF WEST END   Peter Freund

WHEN THE GODS COME HOME TO ROOST   Marc Estrin

WHIRLIGIG   Christopher Salerno

WHITE, CHRISTIAN   Christopher Stoddard

WINTER LETTERS   Vasyl Makhno

WITHIN THE SPACE BETWEEN   Stacy Cartledge

A WORLD OF NOTHING BUT NATIONS   Tod Thilleman

A WORLD OF NOTHING BUT SELF-INFLICTION   Tod Thilleman

WOULD-BE WAND   Robert Podgurski

WRECKAGE OF REASON   (ed.) Nava Renek